Epiphany
(the American)

Lx Milarre

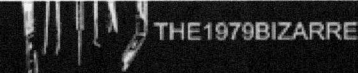

Published 2014

First Printing: 2014

ISBN 978-0-692-27131-5

THE 1979 BIZARRE
Seattle, WA
www.the1979bizarre.com

To My Past Self

Unfiltered
Unedited

-ONE-

There was yellowish snot dribbling out of the pudgy little runt's nostrils and running down his lips. I'm sorry. I didn't see your dog. He, he came out of nowhere! What's so special about the Grand Canyon, it's just a big ditch? This is what twenty bucks will get you nowadays? A couple crusty sandwiches, a shot of vodka and a photo of Jesus Christ. This is nothing! The four old men were lined up side by side for their bowling team photo till one of their heads exploded. I understand the polar ice caps are melting, and fast, but can I still get ice cubes? Wake up, you're about to have your epiphany. When does the show start? I've got to be at work by nine am or I'll miss out on another day of regret.

"Epiphany, my epiphany? Who said that?" Did the words come out of my mouth, or did I just say them in my head? I can't feel my body. Everything's cloudy and my head is spinning slowly. There must be rain

cause I can feel water splashing all over my face. It's hot and salty.

It takes me a couple seconds to fully wake up, and when I open my eyes all the way I'm laying on my back looking straight up at some ratty old man's wiener pissing all over me. "What the hell!" I half shout trying to shift my body to dodge his stream of urine. "Hey, hey! Cut it out. I'm sleeping here!"

The old man doesn't even hear me. He's just standing there staring straight ahead while letting the last of his piss dribble out.

I didn't notice it at first, but moving any part of my body sends sharp pains ping-ponging around inside me. I should have put more padding between me and the pavement. Now I'd be stiff all day. The old man had stopped pissing but was still standing motionless over where I'd setup camp the night before.

There wasn't much lighting here last night, but I thought I had chosen a pretty good private spot where I wouldn't be disturbed and I could sleep alone. Now that the daylight filled the alley around me, I could see piles of dingy soiled fabrics and papers with body's shifting around under them. I'd walked right into a nest of homeless bums and their litter of beer bottles, used newspapers and pieces of random salvaged trash decorated the alley.

"Um, excuse me? Do you think maybe, you could um," I didn't get a chance to finish talking to the old pisser standing above me letting his wiener just hang there and drip all over my sleeping spot. Halfway through my sentence he just sort of looked like he was going to lean forward, like to get a close look at the wall, but just kept going. The old heap of dirty flesh and cloth collapsed on me!

"Aghhhh!" The pains shooting through my body as I scrambled to get out from under the weight of this thing were killing me, along with a smell worse than any pile of garbage. "Oh God, help me!" I tried to shout but was muffled by the guy's greasy long hair. How could this guy weight so much, shouldn't the homeless be all scrawny and boney from not eating? Why was this guy a million pounds? I couldn't move, he had me pinned and my strength was gone.

I felt my life slipping and I was struggling to breath, I pictured some cop walking his beat would find my body buried under this monster of filth. What a way to go, born in a prestigious hospital on the North side, and suffocated to death by a random homeless guy in the South side, what a life.

I closed my eyes and accepted my fate, trying hard to picture the life I was living just a few days earlier to try and escape the harsh reality of my last moments of life. An apartment, wife and kids. Pushing my brain to see every detail of my wife Melanie's face. The cute dimples and that crinkle between her brow when she smiles.

And just like that. Like a surgeon pulling a bullet from your gut, or a fireman plucking you from the third floor of a burning building, some strange gorilla of a homeless man pulled that lump of contaminated flesh off my body and saved my life. Half shocked and half too weak to move, I just lay there. While the good Samaritan homeless jumped around the old pisser and then flung himself on top of me and pressed his scratchy unshaven lips against mine and blew bits of something and hot air into my mouth.

Oh dear God he was trying to give me rescue breaths! I flapped my arms and kicked my legs, like a kid having a temper tantrum. I'd choose the suffocation death from the old pisser over this gorilla giving me mouth to mouth any day.

As the gorilla pulled back to take a breath for himself I slipped my hand in between our lips before he could give another blow.

"You all right? You all right man?" he hobbled off of me, being sure to use my rib cage as support in giving himself a boost. "Hey, you all right?"

I couldn't answer and shut him up cause I was coughing my lungs up. Jesus Christ what the hell kind of toxic air did that guy blow into me? I lifted myself up into a sitting position and shooed the gorilla away while I hacked out the last of the contaminated air.

"You all right, eh?" he kept blabbering.

"Yeah, yeah. I'm good." Yeah right! Like hell I was. My second night on the street, third day away from home. Haven't eaten more than a handful of crackers in days. Unemployed with no more than a couple bucks in my pocket, last time I checked at least . The same dirty clothes on my back as when I left home. Oh Jesus and home. A whole family that has no clue I'm even alive and here in the city. They're probably at my funeral right now wondering where the body that should be in the coffin is. Christina's probably there too, that bitch! I wonder if her and Melanie will do more than glare at each other?

I did my best to stretch out my sore limbs and get into a comfortable sitting position.

"Holy Jesus! You killed Pappy!" some craggily voice shouted.

"Oh man, this isn't good. We're all going to hell now," shouted another.

Dirty men covered head to toe in ratty old clothes were crawling out from every corner of the alley and creeping slowly towards me and the old pisser laying on the ground.

"You killed him man. Murdered him with your cold hearted hands. I saw it!"

"Yeah I saw him to. Choked old Pappy to death."

I couldn't tell who was saying what. There must have been a dozen of them all huddled around me like some kinda grisly football team from the sewers, getting their stink all over. One of them stuck their arm out and shoved me. Then another and another. I was too weak to shove back, let alone get to my feet. "No! Wait," I tried to shout. A weathered old ball of a fist with dirty nails and hairy knuckles came out from the small mob of pathetic rags and flesh, and landed square on my eye.

That was all it took to knock me on my back, but it wasn't enough for our fearless friends. They mustered up their strength together and lifted me, spare my good newspapers, up like royalty. However I was far from royalty in their eyes. Nevertheless all I could do was curl into a ball and wait as they all carried me above their heads towards the end of the alley where they launched me onto the sidewalk, just a few inches from the edge of the curb and speeding traffic.

I wasn't close to any of them, never even saw their faces before, but I couldn't help but feel abandoned. Like some kid whose parents just threw out of the house and left to the carneys. So just like that, I crawled to a pole where I hoisted myself up, dusted my clothes off, cracked my back, took a deep breath of diesel, swallowed my shame and walked down one of the many pathetic streets of life.

I passed hoodlums and businessmen, models and hookers. It was just one piece of walking trash after another. One set of legs carried waste on the outside while the next was rotting away inside. I could see right through the polyester sport coats and the push up bras, their cold hearts were wrapped tightly in wads of blood soaked cash. I stopped and leaned on parking meters, garbage cans, people, walls and even a dog for strength. But they couldn't hold me up long, either I'd slip right off or they would move out from under me and I'd end up on the ground again covered in filth.

There was a railing and I hung over it and waited for the puke to come up, but my stomach was empty and dry heaving was the best I could do. Something had poisoned my mind and reality was folding up around me. The whole damn mess of a city was nothing but a blur. Every building and face look just like the one my eyes had just come off of. Everything just kinda swirled together and became a big gray headache with a shot of car fumes.

I must have staggered only a couple of blocks but it felt like I covered the whole the city and back. Every muscle in my body ached and it felt like my bones were deteriorating by the second. I could feel my brain turn to soup and slosh around between my ears. I had no energy left to blink. So when my knees buckled and my body stumbled through the nearest doorway like a drunk, it was no surprise the little Chinese shop owner treated me like the rest of the scum on the street. He threatened to call the cops and grabbed his little broom and tried to sweep me back out the door. Like a dead cockroach or a cigarette butt. But my body was too big and heavy for this little man and his broom. The little stick with bristles like wires cracked in half which sent the man into an uproar and caused the little old Chinese woman in the back to come out yelling and shaking her fists. And between the two of them yelling about some yin this and yang that and me getting kicked in the ribs by each of them, I passed out.

Maybe it would have been better just to stay passed out, or even have been murdered in my sleep. But that's just wishful thinking. When I recovered, both my consciousness and my recollection, I found myself folded up in the fetal position in a bathtub. I waited a little while, knowing that as soon as I moved the aches and pains would return.

After a good ten minutes of moving like some old man with brittle bones, I was able to crawl out of the tub and sit on this rusted toilette. Only now was I able to take in the shit hole that surrounded me through one eye, the other was swollen shut thanks to that homeless fellow with the big fist.

This looked like some kinda bathroom you'd find in a prison, or a fucking hobo shack. The tile walls were all cracked up, along with the stained floor. The toilette and sink looked institution like cause they were both made of silver metal and all dinged up. There was a cracked mirror that looked permanently fogged over. Even the bathtub stall couldn't escape the worn out look of this room. What was left of the torn up brittle plastic curtain hung in shreds sadly from the rusted curtain pole and added a spooky horror show feel to the tub with brown water rings below. I could just imagine Psycho taking place in there. And the only way I could see any of this was because thank God there was a small spider-web covered window up near the ceiling. Bless the dusty light that illuminates my personal hell.

"Where the fuck am I?" I thought out loud. Even famous

13

philosophers couldn't compete with my bewilderment. As soon as these bones stop aching I'll drink some water out of the sink. My throat is beyond dry.

After a couple seconds of pulling at the cold water handle I got frustrated and yanked the hot water one, only to have brown water trickle out of the faucet. Hell, it was better than nothing. I drank at the little stream like it was the fountain of youth. I felt like some dog lapping at a broken sprinkler head, but who cares?

"You up?" someone on the other side of the door yelled out and pounded on the door. "Hey! You awake mister?"

I remembered the little Chinese woman and massaged my bruised ribs. It was her.

"Hey mister!" she yelled again.

"Yeah, what?"

"You awake?"

"What do you think?" I said.

There was silence and then, "What are you doing?"

"Taking a bath and giving myself a pedicure," what the hell kinda questions are these?

"Don't get smart! Or you won't eat."

Eat? Did she just say eat? "Food? You can give me food?" I said. I couldn't believe it. I almost forgot what food was I haven't eaten in so long. Yesterday was my third day without food and after a while the burning in the stomach just fades away and you forget about it. "I would really appreciate it if you could give me something. I haven't eaten in days and I'm very hungry." I tried my best to sound non-threatening, and get some sympathy across.

"You hungry, eh? I have food for you but one thing," she waited for me to answer.

"Yes?"

"Food not free. You'll have to do something for us."

"Yeah sure. Whatever, I'll clean your bathroom." Just give me some food little woman.

"No. Sun will tell you when he gets back," she said.

Sun? That must be her courageous little husband, the one with the broom, well busted broom anyway. "Ok, ok just give me some food right now or I might die," I said not even having to force myself to sound like a weak man in need of nourishment. "Please."

I let my head fall into the sink and listened to her feet shuffle as she walked away from the door. I hope she brings meat.

Two, no three, days on the streets and you turn into an animal scrambling to survive. The city becomes your man made jungle. You forget everything you learned about manners and civilization as you know it doesn't exist anymore. You hunt for your food just like your cave-dwelling ancestors. Digging for leftovers in dumpsters like your hairy head-to-toe great-grandfather picked through bushes for berries. But water always comes first and you're always on the look out for a thin stream of brown liquid flowing from a crack in a pipe or a wall. Even if it's running down the gutter and has yellow foam, drink it! Dark corners, like caves, become your best friend. They provide protection and you hide, sleep, drink, piss and shit in there. Every human becomes an enemy and you fend for yourself trusting no one, all language skills disappear and grown men resort to growling and fist fights. At night you scrounge for the safest spot, avoiding anything that breaths like the plague. In the end you're one step away from cannibalism eyeing up the other bi-pedal beasts around you. I hope she brings meat.

I hadn't meant to go this far. I didn't think this would ever happen. What the hell was I thinking? Was I even thinking? I let the freshest water I had drank in days dribble down my head and neck while I leaned into the sink. Was this all worth it? Leaving the family and life I had know for so long behind, for this: dirty water and near starvation.

There was a tap on the door and then the little woman's voice, "Foods here. Come get it."

When I tried to open the door it was locked. "I can't open the door."

"No, under the door," she said.

"Huh?" I stepped back and looked at the bottom of the door. A yellowish paper towel slipped halfway out from the gap under the door. I watched as a thin slice of bread was pushed under the door on top of the towel. Then another slice. I had to squat down slowly to pick up the pieces of food as they came through. Two slices of bread, some wilted lettuce, a couple slices of cheese and then there it was. A little dry and discolored, yet the bologna made me salivate harder then ever in my life. I snatched it out from under the door before she could finish pushing it.

"You really hungry, eh?" she asked giving a little laugh at the end.

I couldn't even answer I had already swallowed the bologna and half the cheese.

"There's a sink in there if you need to drink," she said. "Sun will be here soon, then you will come out. Remember you promised you'd do something."

I put the bread and lettuce in my mouth took a couple bites and swallowed them. Shit I could eat the paper towel, and I actually considered it. Sun, sun, sunshine will you ever come out and wash away the rain?

It wasn't hard to tell when Sun arrived. The whole place was quiet as a library until he walked through the door. With all the silence and losing daylight from the window, I was beginning to think I was stuck in sensory deprivation. First there was the sound of a door slamming, even though it was muffled. Then fast voices that turned into short yells like an argument and then cut off abruptly. I had my head pressed up against the door, but I still couldn't make out a word.

I strained my eardrums for a sound, anything even a whisper. Then I heard it, actually I felt it more. Footsteps, soft and slow. Someone, or both of them, could be felt and barely heard walking very slowly into the room on the other side of the door. Walking right up to the door, and finally I felt a slight push against my head as pressure was applied to the other side of the door. Someone was pressing their head right up to the door trying to listen to me.

I thought about how less than an inch of wood and cranium separated my brain from theirs. If only I could force my neurons to jump out my ear slip between the fiber in the wood, crawl up their ear canal and take over their brain I could unlock the door and get the hell out of here.

Come on speak. What are you going to do to me? What are you waiting for? I thought about laying on the floor and playing dead.

There was a light knock, almost polite like. But then the voice ruined it.

"Hey," it was a man's voice. "Hello, are you awake?" His tense voice was right on the other side of the door. So, it was *his* head pressing up against it.

What would happen if I didn't answer? "Yeah, I'm up," I answered after stepping back away from the door.

"My wife said she gave you food. Did you eat it?"

"Yeah, it wasn't much but I'm thankful," I really don't want to make any enemies so I tried to remain polite, even though it was his and his wife's feet that put the sore purple blotches all over my torso.

He seemed to understand my purpose and his voice relaxed. "Ok, good. Then you agreed to do something for us, right?"

"Yeah," I had to hold back from asking for more food, but my stomach was begging me.

"Look, we don't care if you're a drugger or homeless or steal from other people," the man started to say but then his wife cut him off.

"But don't steal from us!" she cut in quickly.

"Shh," I heard the husband whisper harshly.

"Yes, don't steal from us I have a gun," he said.

"Don't worry. I'm harmless. I won't steal from you or try to hurt you. I'm just a desperate man without a home right now. I'm not a drug user or a thief. I'll repay you for the sandwich," I waited a minute then added, "and if you want to give me another I wouldn't mind."

"You ate the last meats and cheese!" the wife said.

Again the harsh "Shh!" came from the husband followed by something in Chinese.

"We are going to need your help. With something," he started. "We have a daughter. She has. Out daughter needs our help, someone's help."

The Chinese man was speaking in fragments, like he was too afraid too just come out and say what he wanted. "What's wrong with your daughter?" I asked.

The man didn't answer, but instead began moving latches and things from the other side of the door. After a few clicks and snaps, the door knob slowly started to turn and the door creaked open.

A bleak stream of light slipped between the door and the wall, ran along the tile floor and fell on the toilette next to me.

"Where, where are you?" the woman asked.

"Step into the light," said the man.

Feeling ashamed like a bad dog or a punished child I step into the light and faced the little couple that only hours ago put dents in my sides. I stood a good two feet taller than them and yet I still felt smaller. We stared at each other through the crack for one of those uncomfortable silent moments.

I couldn't see every detail, but I could tell they were either really old, or maybe middle aged and just looked old and weathered, like a pair of used up gloves, all wrinkly, dry and cracked up. No matter what, life hadn't been good to these folks. Their faces were all scrunched up and what was left of their hair was all scraggily and thinned out. Even their eyes had sunken back into their skulls, like little round turtle heads that have been scared back into the shell. This little couple looked as though they were born and then pushed through time at an ultra high speed until finally here they were standing in front me, a tall, healthy for the most part, American brought up on cheap convenient store sugar cakes and green plastic toy soldiers. Their clothes looked as bad off as them, probably hand-me-downs from the founding generation of China. And of course they were short, really short, like garden gnomes come to life. Authentic Chinese here in downtown, living in some kinda shit hole, guessing by the state of their bathroom.

They didn't say a word, God only knows what they were thinking. We just stood their staring until the man told me he had a gun again and then said they really needed my help, again. He unbuckled the last safety latch with shaky hands and asked me to come out slowly and not to make any fast moves. The wife was obviously frightened ducking behind her husband for protection. I wasn't going to hurt these people. Christ I have kids of my own, well at least had kids in my *old* life. It's hard to imagine this is the same couple that beat me up earlier.

They led me silently through their dimly lit ramshackle of a house or business, I couldn't tell which. There was clutter everywhere, all sorts of stuff too. I could make out lots of barrels with lids on, like they were stockpiling food or something. Boxes and boxes stacked on top of each other in tall crooked pillars that defied physics. I couldn't see it, but could imagine all the dust, like a fuzzy blanket covering everything in sight. We walked down a crazy labyrinth of shit, me following the gnomes. Honestly, I don't know who was more scared at this point, I had no idea where they were taking me or even where I was really, the place was getting darker with each step and the halls were getting smaller.

My brain's telling me to just turn and run for it. I know the old man's shitting me when he says he has a gun. But the heart part of me feels I should keep my word and help their daughter, and the stomach part of me wants another sandwich. Two against one. I'll stick with them.

Just when I was thinking I would be too big to get past the next turn we stopped. The man looked at me and then opened a door that I didn't even know was there. The woman ducked into the room and the man closed the door and waited outside with me. We didn't say a word, but listened to the sound of something coming from inside the room. My eyes had finally adjusted to the darkness and I'm not sure, but I think I could see a tear coming from the man's eyes?

The door opened again, this time from the inside. The man looked at me and said in a low voice, "Remember, you promised to help us." Then he stepped inside and motioned for me to follow. I don't know what the big deal was, it was probably something simple. I crouched down and entered the room.

When I lifted my head it took a moment for everything to register, and even then it didn't make much sense. First of all the lighting wasn't much better in here, there were no windows and the only thing lighting the room was coming from what looked like a pile of candles all melted into a small pile on a box. The room wasn't much bigger than the bathroom I was trapped in all day, and just as shabby. The walls, if you could call them that, looked home-made. They were really just like sheets of wood nailed together. Actually it looked like the whole damn room was just patches of shit nailed together.

I didn't realize it at first, but besides the husband, wife and me, there was another body in the room. Their daughter of course. If it was the daughter, she was sitting in a little doll-house like chair with her back to me and the door. Her parents had moved to each side of her and stood there like they were guarding her or something.

The mom spoke first, "You can't leave now."

Then the dad interrupted, "No, no you promised. Don't leave." He sounded more pathetic and desperate than ever. "Please. We really need your help."

"Our daughter," the mom started but didn't finish.

21

It was hard to pay attention to what they were trying to say. I was too busy being scared shitless thinking the walls were going to cave in any second and I'd be trapped in here like a miner. Where was the door? I looked around anxiously but somehow the door disappeared, everything on the walls blended into each other. It was getting hot and hard to breathe in here and I felt claustrophobia setting in.

"Ok, ok what is it? I'll help you just tell me what you want?" who cares if I sounded impatient or demanding. I was beginning to think this wasn't worth a stale sandwich. Then my eyes fell on their eyes again, those sad, helpless, child like eyes trapped in the old gnomes. "I'm sorry, I didn't mean to sound so, I don't know. I'm just not feeling well in here. Could we please hurry?" I waited a second, "Why is your daughter sitting backwards?"

"Mister, you have to help us. Our daughter needs it," the mother said sounding like she was on the verge of tears.

"You keep saying that. You aren't telling me what exactly you need." I took a step towards the little girl sitting down and reached out to touch her shoulder.

"Stop!" the father shouted and jumped at my arm. The wife wrapped her arms around her daughter and hugged her tight. The dad got his energy back he started talking, and fast. "Don't touch her! No, no. Step back we'll tell you. Our daughter has a problem, problems. We don't know what but we need help," he paused for a moment. "Step back, we'll show you. You'll see," he said anxiously.

Jesus Christ what the hell is this man talking about? A problem with his daughter what am I suppose to do? What is it like a behavior problem? Is she some rotten teenager who can't stand this shit hole and tries to escape all the time? I don't blame her. Screw the heart and stomach I want to leave this place, now.

I was almost backed up against the wall and the mom started whispering something into the girl's ear. The girl nodded and the mother let go of her daughter's boney shoulders. I don't know what was going on, I felt like I was in some sort of private movie theater watching these miniature people move around. The mom and dad embracing as the daughter stood up slowly. And I thought the parents were small, this girl was half the size of them. All the movement started making the candle light flicker to stay lit, even more like a private movie theater. The dad pulling the chair out of the way. Finally after forever the girl turned around and faced me.

Don't ever kid yourself into thinking grown men don't scream. A loud sound came out of me. I screamed from my stomach and couldn't stop. It was like a switch was thrown inside my mind and all the screams I had held in all my life finally came out like a siren.

As soon as my first yell came up the mom put the candle out and the room went pitch black. I only had a glimpse of the girl once she turned around, but that was all I needed. The image was burned into my mind and it was almost as though I was still looking at her.

Oh God I wish she was just a rotten, disobedient kid. Kid, kid! That wasn't even a kid! Wasn't even human! What the hell was that thing? Oh dear God get me out of here, this is a horrible nightmare. Get me the fuck out of this place!

The room was completely black and I couldn't see a thing. I was yelling uncontrollably like my lungs had a life of their own and all they wanted to do was push air out as hard and as fast as they could. I swung

23

my arms around me. I didn't want that thing coming near me, and I wanted to find the door as fast as I could. I smacked into all sorts of things, hard and soft. If my hands were bleeding or messed up I couldn't tell and didn't care.

Someone else started screaming, it was high pitched and sounded like a deranged animal. There was shouting in Chinese. Oh Jesus something just ran into me! Oh God I am fucking freaking out! Fuck, fuck, fuck! I'm trapped in a room with this shrunken thing, what if it bites me? What will it do? I swung my arms harder and tried to sweep them across the wall to find a door knob or latch, anything. Nothing, I'm finding nothing and losing my breath from screaming so much.

The image of the thing flashed across my mind again. It was short and had the body of a little girl wearing a Sunday dress. But the face, the head, oh dear God I wish it weren't true. That wasn't a girls head! What the hell is in this room?

All I could feel was the rough, jagged edges of boards of wood and nail heads sticking out. My eardrums were burning from my yells that kept coming up, the thing's sharp shrieks and all the Chinese shouting. Something small brushed against my side and I freaked out and started running waving my arms in front of me. My knees hit something and I fell forward, into another body and it shouted in pain.

That thing, that face.

Then like Jesus fucking Christ come save the day the door swung open and just enough light for me to make out the hall outside shown through. I scrambled to my feet and dashed for the opening. I didn't stop once I was through the door. I kept running, spare the screaming now, and made my way through the crazy isles of tall shadows. My legs hit boxes and barrels and God knows what else. It was one sharp turn after another, dodging and jumping toward whatever direction held more light. Finally I made it to some sort of wall that I followed until there was a door. I frantically grab at the knob trying to twist it in my sweaty numb hands but something wasn't working right. Either it was my hands or the knob. I gave up and saw a window just a few steps away.

That window was my gateway to sanity. I didn't even bother to unlatch it, just threw a chunk of something next to me at it and crawled through the broken glass frame into a moonlit alley.

I didn't stop running through alleys and streets till I was in the middle of a crowded street filled with normal human bodies with normal human heads. Only then was I able to lean into a doorway and let everything come out, emotions, sweat, tears, and finally the stale sandwich. "Jesus Christ, what the hell was that?" I said out loud to myself.

I walked over to the curb and sat down letting my eyes fall onto the lines of people walking up and down the street like an endless parade. I debated whether or not to go over the recent event in my mind. In the end I figured it would be best to just clear my head and sort it all out later. Right now I needed a break. The past hours have been rough and my mind needed to recover. So just forget what happened, alright.

-TWO-

How long does one have to sit before they can become fully enlightened and understand all that is around them? I let time pass for a good while, while I just stared at the people's legs walking by and threw mindless questions in and out of my mind. The passing legs are hypnotizing, an endless assembly line of swinging feet. Sometimes they bump you, sometimes they kick stuff into you, but most of the time they just walk right past not even noticing you.

It didn't take long for memories of my family to start seeping in. Where are they? What are they doing? What are they thinking? These are silly questions, the answers are obvious. They're at home, probably sitting together talking and thinking about me. Matter of fact, they've probably got more questions about me, than I have of them.

Yeah, well I wish there was some way I could let you know I love you and always have. Yes and you too Melanie. Yes, and I miss you all too.

It's not your fault that I killed myself, well faked it. What I did was for the best of all of us. Don't blame yourselves, I just got myself into too many problems and had no way out. You're all better off now, just forget about me and start your lives over again. You can do it, be strong Melanie. Be strong for the kids and yourself.

It's funny how you can start thinking of something and it turns into a daydream and before you know it, all your senses shut down and everything around you just sort of fades away. Who knows how long I would have sat there and stared off into space if that rock hadn't hit me in the back off the head.

"Who threw that!?" It wasn't really a question, more of a threat. I turned around to face my attacker, but found myself staring at what looked like an old man laying on the ground. It was hard to tell cause he was way back in the alley behind me and there wasn't much lighting.

"I'm sorry, I didn't mean to hurt you," the little man said. "I was calling but you couldn't hear me, so I threw a small rock."

"What do you want?" I asked trying to squint to see clearer.

"I was walking down the steps here and slipped on something. Every time I try to get up, I get a bad pain in my leg and I'm not so young anymore so I think I might have done some damage."

I started to get up and walk cautiously towards him. "I just need some help up, if you wouldn't mind. You look like a strong young one," he continued. Well I was thirty-four, hardly a young one. But as I got closer I could see he was in fact some old looking guy who had fallen down a small set of steps, and his leg looked pretty twisted.

"Oh geez, that doesn't look right," I told him. "Maybe I shouldn't move you and should go get some help?" I started to walk toward a door at the top of the steps he fell down.

"No, no! It's not serious this happens to me a lot. Just help me up and I'll be fine."

I stared at him and back at his leg another moment, "Alright, if you say so." I got a grip on his arm and got into a good lifting position. "Ready, one, two-"

Before I could give the old heave-ho someone's arm swung around my neck and another pinned one of my arms.

The old man jumped up, and now I could tell he wasn't even an old man, just some young guy with a beard maybe painted white or something. "Alright bastard, take this. Hold 'em Jimmy" And he slugged in me in the gut.

I didn't even have a full breath of air in me, so as soon as his fist smashed into me I was doubling over and gasping for air. The thing behind me let go and I was free to stand on my own, but I wasn't doing a good job. I could see the two of them now laughing then one kicked my shin so I had to hop around till I grabbed the railing for support.

"I, I" hard to get air still, "don't have, have anything. No money. Poor." Jesus was it hard to talk.

"Money? Did ya' hear that Jimmy this distinguished gentleman here thinks we want his dough!" the old man looking one said laughing.

Then the other started in, "We don't want yr money, kind sir. We got our own bucks."

I was barely getting my breath back, "Then, what do you want, with me?" I asked slowly.

"Want with ya? We don't wan'cha at all Mister," one of them said. "We hate the homeless, think y're nothin' but trash."

"Yeah, wastes of space. Worthless as the stray cats that prowl the back alleys an' the shit they leave behind," said the other tough guy, "Meow". He stuck his tongue out and flicked it at me.

They were doubling up on me, and forcing me to back up the steps the old man tricked me into thinking he fell down. I didn't have enough breath to yell to the front of the alley where all the people were.

"This wont take long. Naw we promise to be quick, just close yr eyes an' count to ten if ya' know how."

My back was now up against the door. The man that strangled me reached behind his back and pulled out something that looked like a red stained paddle with rusted razor blades sticking out of it. The other, old man, guy just kept smiling his crooked smile and looking nuts while creeping towards me, "Come 'ere pussy, pussy."

I could feel the doorknob pushing against my back and before I could even debate whether to attempt opening it or not, I had already turned around, swung open the door and slipped through.

They put up a fight, pulling on the door from the other side, but I managed to shut the door long enough for me to lock it.

Safe from the hounds banging away at the door, I now found myself trapped in some dark, narrow hallway. The sound of extremely loud bass was thudding down the hall and through my ear canal pounding away at my brain. What is this, some club? Outside I never bothered to see what building I was sitting next to the whole time, but I knew the area was filled with nocturnal people, so a club sounds about right.

This wouldn't be too bad, I'll just work my way to the front, try not to be noticed and then I can slip out the front door or something. I guess

29

that plan would have worked out fine, if I was in was one of those regular dancing clubs. But after the hallway and some winding turns and another door I found myself walking a mirrored corridor lined with doors and flashing red lights. Every angle you looked there were more you's, more doors and even more red light, not to mention the thudding bass was louder. This was a fucking epileptic's seizure waiting to happen.

But that's ok, I can deal with the endless images of myself degenerating into some sort of street rat. What triggered my precaution was every time I passed a door, sounds of women screaming could be heard from the other side. I didn't stop to listen until I got to the end of the hall. Then I put my ear up to the last door and listened to what sounded like carnal hell.

There was a man's voice saying something, I couldn't make out what, and a woman letting out yelps and screams like an animal. Something sounded like metal making loud clicks and snaps, maybe sparks. Jesus Christ what kind of sadistic shit is going on in there? I didn't want to stick around and find out, so I made a dash down the hall hoping the next door I'd open would lead to the exit.

Wrong again. The next door opened to what you could say was the club, or main room. Booming music poured out of every direction and bright swirling lights in the distance kept blinding me. The bass was so loud it was like being in a room with a giant speaker for a heart pumping sound waves of blood through the adjourning hallway veins. I ducked into a dark area up against the wall to avoid being seen and let my body absorb the music's vibrations.

In front of me there was no dance floor, only rows of benches, like pews, filled mostly with men and in front of them is something of an altar only there was no priest speaking the word of the lord. Instead a tall, skinny black man dressed like a cross between Dracula and Liberace was getting down and singing a lot of "yeah, yeah, yeahs," while humping the air around him. It was an overdone special effects stage for the church of rejected disco.

I had a good spot for sneaking out, the audience all had the back of their heads to me and were focused on the jumpin' black man, and I was in a dark enough area that anyone else wouldn't see me unless they knew I was here. All I had to do was keep my back against the wall so I could squeeze through the narrow gap between the last pew and the wall and slowly creep my way to what looks like the entrance about thirty feet away.

Inch by inch I slid myself along the back wall, this wasn't so bad it might take a while but I'll get there. I half amused myself by watching the energetic black priest preach about makin' love to the wrong woman tied up in all the right places'. He couldn't sing for shit, it was more like shrieking. Anyway, you had to admit the guy was a good dancer, jumping around his altar and even throwing in some break dancing moves. The audience was totally transfixed by this cosmic, gothic, sinful singing priest, they could have passed for zombies with their dead stares.

I can't believe I've only gone a few feet, this was really harder than it looked. In some places the gap between the wall and the pew was so narrow I had to suck in my gut to get by. I looked ahead to see how much further I had to go. Shit! I didn't notice before, unless the guy just got here, but there was someone in the last row. Was he there before? I would have noticed. He's there now and that's all that matters. There's no way I could get past without him noticing. Shit! Shit! Shit! Well, he's halfway between me and the end, a good 25 feet. Maybe he'll leave soon?

I decided to keep up my pace and hope for the best. Meanwhile the black dancer kept up his own pace and now had smoke machines going off around him. This only added to his divine appearance, making him look like some kind of black angel among the clouds, humping of course.

And this must be his backup. Rows of heads slowly started emerging from the smoky area around him. One by one pale, rail thin girls dressed head to toe in skimpy black leather outfits with collars, marched out like an S&M army trained by Hitler himself. The black priest kept his beat and I kept my inching. A minute later I was a few feet closer to the end, and the altar was loaded with the Nazi dolls. What kind of show is this? Now that they were out of the smoky stuff, I could see all the girls were handcuffed together and lined up.

Ok whatever they're preparing for, the girls don't look like they're looking forward to it. It looks like they might have been crying or something. They all have black mascara and makeup that was running down their cheeks and all smudged up. These girls looked like they just crawled out of hell, and from the expressions on their faces, they were headed back. But the priest of darkness kept dancing, the zombies kept staring and I kept inching.

Ok, good news and bad news. Good, I was now about halfway to the end, only fifteen more feet. Bad, I was only four feet away from our friend in the back row. If he were to just rotate his zombie head a fraction of an inch he'd see me. I had to keep my back flat up against the wall and breathe like a guy in a coma, any move might catch the guy's attention. I even blinked less, even though it didn't matter. I've turned into one of the lifeless zombies in front of me. There is absolutely no way I could slip behind this guy without bumping his head or something.

What's the worst that could happen if I'm caught? I mean come on, all that could happen is they'd say 'oh my God, how'd you get in?' and a big guy would come and escort me out. Right? Ok, so wait and see if he moves, or make a sound and get caught. Wait, or make a sound? Wait or make a sound?

While I was contemplating my course of action and riding the sound vibrations off the wall, things had changed on the altar. Instead of his regular erratic dancing, the priest was slowly slinking around the girls licking at them and threatening to bite them all over.

Shit, I wandered into some sort of triple x show, that's what this is. Okay, dance around with the girls, strip them, maybe screw a couple and call it a night. Maybe I could stick this out? It'd be the best entertainment all week. I started missing Christina. God those were good times.

The dolls stood stiff and didn't flinch when the priest flung his arms in front of their faces, missing them by inches. He kept dancing around them striking out menacingly at them and coming close to scratching and hitting them, but never actually coming into contact. The girls didn't even blink, just stood their ground and stared back at the zombies.

I studied everything closely never moving an inch, just letting my eyeballs roll around in their sockets and take everything in like spy cameras. I watched as the perverted priest started humping towards the girls and growling. I watched the zombies watch the priest, and I made sure to keep the corner of my eye on the backseat stranger. The music and bass were still pumping hard and my ear drums were stinging causing my hearing to fade.

Out of the ceiling somewhere a bright spot light flew across the zombie heads, swinging back and forth before stopping on one in particular. He stood up as if summoned by some magical spell, or somehow had the gift of life passed on to him through the intense light. Then the zombie slowly walked toward the altar as if in a trance, dragging something behind him. The spotlight stayed fixed on him, making him the brightest thing in sight.

I could only see the back of him, business suit with a good build underneath. He probably wasn't bad looking, a normal guy. He finally made it to the line of dolls and stood at one end with his back to the audience. It was hard to see, but it looked like he put his arm out and attached the thing he was dragging to the collar on her neck. A leash. Ok, so maybe the audience gets in on this. An interactive show.

The priest danced his way over to the two of them and uncuffed the girl so she was free from the other dolls, but now in complete submission to this white collar zombie. The zombie led his new slave doll back into the smoke at the back of the altar and they both disappeared.

The spotlight slid back down the altar toward the audience and began it's wild back and forth movement again, swinging across the audience. It stopped on another zombie head and he arose just like the first, in a trance. I watched as he repeated the same actions as the first zombie, like they were all trained for this and just performing their job. One by one the zombies were brought to life from the beam of light, and one by one the frightened girls were led off the altar by their new masters.

Okay, so it's some kinky show, probably even a whore house. Nothing wrong with that. Men have primal urges and your modern housewife armed with her 409 and bed time stories just can't satisfy what evolution has programmed into the instinctual male mind to enforce survival of the species. I don't care what phylum you're in, when a male mammal wants to fuck, he wants to fuck. If a male grabs a passing female and screws her silly in the wild it's called nature, here in man's land it's called rape. So we're forced to restrain ourselves and it only works for so long. I mean the housewife cooks, cleans and manages the munchkins, maybe spends too much time in front of the tube, and she's great for it. So it's not her fault she's just 'too tired' at night. But jerk off privileges can only hold the frustration back so far. Start with non-stop hormones, throw in a couple pornos and a lousy fifteen minute screw once a weekend; mix it all together with a culture pushing sex appeal with every billboard you pass, magazine page you turn and commercial you watch and let the whole fucking thing boil for 10 years and you've got one blue-balled husband ready to use his aching hard-on as a sword to kill for a piece of prime pussy.

After the vows, man is supposed to share his bed with one woman for the rest of his married life, for ever and ever. Till the end of time. Whatever Father McAllister. Maybe on an island where it's one woman per man, or if you only lived to the age of 35. But honestly, 50 years in bed with the same pussy that just gets older, drier and staler with each passing night. Trust me, Dr. Frankenstein and 1,000 volts of electricity couldn't bring my wife's expired twat back to life. The beaver's deader than my childhood dog. The only solution is to go find a substitute and keep your fingers crossed the old lady doesn't find out, at least till you get too old to get it up.

I did it to save our marriage; I did it to save myself. If Christina hadn't come along, I'd be in a padded cell. I probably wouldn't have put up with Melanie and the kids for as long as I did.

I don't blame these guys, if it saves the family and the wife doesn't find out, then cheat away my friends. And if you're single, all the better. But I still couldn't get over those faces on the girls. Something just wasn't right.

My eardrums couldn't take the pounding anymore and finally shutdown. It was like someone just flipped a switch and all sound just shut off. I could still feel the wall and air vibrating with the beat, but what happened next I could only witness through a silent world.

The next guy showed me why the girls looked so disturbed. After he clipped his leash to her and her cuffs were released, she panicked or something. The girl tried to resist being pulled into the smoke and even let herself fall on the floor. I couldn't hear a thing, but her mouth was opening and closing like she was yelling, so something must have been coming out. Then her makeup started running all over the place, she was crying hard.

The unholy priest that would never see a cloud in heaven then, right in front of everyone, smacked the girl. Then again and again, even kicking her. All the girls in the line tried their hardest not to cringe, and the zombies just stared. The girl curled up into a ball while the priest kicked her like a busted tire. Finally some giant of a guy stomped halfway out of the smoke, grabbed the leash from the zombie and dragged the poor girl off the smoking altar kicking and screaming. Those girls really are going back to hell!

What kind of place is this? Christ! Someone should do something. How can they let this happen? Right before my eyes the disco altar had turned into some twisted torture chamber for these young girls. I want to jump over these pews right now and save that poor girl. What are they doing to her back there? My mind raced with ideas and shock over what I just witnessed. Complete and utter shock. I didn't even notice the spotlight had stopped on our zombie friend in the back row this time and I was included in the light.

My hearing still gone, I watched as the zombie heads in the room silently turned an impossible 180 degrees and faced me. Every single one of them pointed in my direction and for the first I could see their faces. Long, gaunt pale faces with two large, solid black eyes embedded above their cheeks. Whites of their eyes? There was no 'whites of their eyes'! They were solid black. I found myself jumping from one face to next desperately trying to find a normal set of eyes in the crowd.

There was nothing I could do. I was completely wedged between the pew and the wall. The priest stopped dancing and the zombies and girls stared straight at me. The priest was shouting something but hell if I could hear him. It was a silent movie with no captions.

I had been in the tight place so long, my waist down had gone numb. I wiggled my upper body as hard as I could, but it was useless. I was seriously stuck. But at the rate I was sweating, it wouldn't be long before ten pounds of saltwater leaked out of me. I started breathing hard and felt my heart beating in my neck. Okay, okay, stop panicking and think this thing out. The priest is yelling at you and God knows what these bug eyed zombies are thinking. Fuck the girl, save yourself. I wiggled and sweated harder.

I don't know where he came from, but the giant who dragged that girl off suddenly ran down the pew towards me, and another brute of a guy followed him. I couldn't hear a thing, I could only watch as they charged at me with ugly, snarling faces like bulls. They each grabbed an arm and I felt something in between my shoulder blades pop when they pulled me up. They wrestled me halfway out, and I honestly don't know if this was a good thing or a bad thing. God knows I wanted out of this place, but part of me was terrified of what these guys could, would do to me considering how they treat ladies.

I opened my mouth and squeezed the air out of my lungs trying hard to yell 'stop', but my eardrums were so busted I don't know what came out of my mouth. They only pulled harder and I felt all the blood leave my head. I glanced quickly around the room at the insect-like eyes wishing the zombies would snap out of their trance and help me.

Something inside me cracked as the thugs gave one last tug and yanked my body free from the gap. Oh please, please don't hurt me. I couldn't say it, but the words were running circles in my head. No kicks, no punches, no blood. Just take me to the front and toss me to the curb. I'm sorry for coming here. Oh God am I sorry.

All I could do was stare back at those slick, shinny black eyes. The giant carried my limp body over his shoulder back the way I came in. Through the door leading to the hall of mirrors and tortured bondage girls. He moved so fast, it was almost like falling. I wanted screamed back at my reflection bouncing quickly down the hall. Once he winded through the dark halls he kicked open the door I had once used to for sanctuary. This place was the furthest thing from sanctuary.

Still unable to hear a thing, I watched my assailants encounter the two pricks that first lured me into the alley. They were roughing up some other poor bum and for a flash of a second I got to see the razor paddle that would have torn me to shreds take half the face off the crusty bum.

The giants dropped me on the asphalt and scared off the two pricks. Then they returned for the kill. Oh dear God please don't kill me. I was scared shitless and the nerves that made my muscles work had short circuited. All I could do was stare. They hovered above me like towers, with giant meaty faces. Their legs and arms were the size of my whole body.

They stared at me for while, probably trying to figure out what to break first. And I stared back, trying to figure out *what* they were going to break first. One of them reached for my arm. No! No! Not my arm, please! I'm just some innocent guy, I'm homeless. The giant lifted me clear off the ground and dangled me like a rag doll. The other brute looked like he was going to use me as a punching bag but then walked over to a dumpster and pulled out a piece of rebar. Oh shit, I'm not going to be alive after this. Just one whack from this guy and I'll go into shock then they'll kill me while I'm unconscious.

I watched the meaty face crack a twisted smile and flex his muscles. Ok, am I supposed to pray? Do I thank God or something about now? I wished I could just close my eyes and get it over with, but my nerves were shot, nothing worked right, not even my eyelids. Just as I thought the brute would swing the bar into me shattering my ribs and life, the giant who was holding me up flung me on my stomach on top of a trashcan.

At least now I couldn't see when the bar would come down. Alright you sons-a-bitches do it and get it over with. No, no I mean don't kill me please. In my mind I braced myself for the sting of the impact. Any second now the bar would come down on my back and cut off all my sensations from the neck down. I'd be paralyzed for a second of my life, then with the next hit I'd be dead. Never having been to church, I started to pray in the only way I knew.

Oh God, thank you for. Thank you for. What do I have to be

thankful for? For this?

I felt something on my lower back but it wasn't the rod. It was the giant's hands and they grabbed at my waist then yanked my pants down. What the hell!? Oh don't tell me! I felt my shorts get ripped off and the hands disappeared. I started praying like I was on speed.

Oh dear God please don't let them rape me. Please don't rape me. Please God, please, please, please. The words shot through my head faster than I could think. God, I know this is weird, but please let them just spank me. Even if it's with the pole, please let that be it.

I felt the pole alright. But it wasn't coming down like a baseball bat on my bare ass. It tore its way right up my asshole and the ice cold rod was only up there a second before it was yanked out. Again and again it was shoved up there. I don't know how long it lasted, but I prayed the whole time. Prayed I never walked into that hell hole, prayed they didn't break anything in me, I just plain prayed they would stop. And finally they did, I don't know if it was out of boredom or what. But I felt the ramming stop and they must have walked away leaving the rod inside me.

Thank you lord! Thank you! Thank you! Don't let them come back. Just give me enough time to get my nerves working again and first thing I'll do is get this rod out of my ass, then crawl off the can and get out of here.

I laid there, draped over the trash can like a dead snake with the rod sticking out of me. I slipped back into my mind and tried to meditate and focus on each muscle in my body. If I could just flip a switch somewhere in my brain and get my freeways of nerves up and running again then rest would be easy. Got to find that switched. I imagined sliding behind the pupils of my eyes and slowly working my way back into my brain and finally that black endless space of the mind. Maybe if I somehow imagine a spark or something and lighting the dark caverns of my skull up like a firework show I could get something working. I tried focusing on brightening the darkness in my head. Then I felt something grab the rod.

Not again. The rod slipped out of my butt and I anticipated its return, but instead felt my pants and shorts work their way back up to my waist. Could they really have had a change of heart? Was it possible for their perverted minds to stop thinking about sodomizing and beating girls long enough to feel sympathy for some poor guy like me? No, they've got to be getting ready for something worse.

My body was rolled off the can and I landed flat on my back into a soft pile of garbage bags. I felt something grab my ankles and start dragging me, but I couldn't see where I was going or who was doing the pulling. They pulled me onto a sheet of cardboard, then continued to pull me. My eyelids were still stuck open and I was forced to watch the tops of dumpsters and brick walls slide by. I even past the unconscious bum with half a face.

And so I was dragged through the alley, my head bumping all the way, till I was put through the uncomfortable position of being pulled up and into the back seat of some compact car. I was crumpled up next to a pile of moldy clothes and forced to stare at my crotch while the compact drove off.

Um, ok. I'm sure those grunts didn't come back to get me cause I was dragged and not carried, but then who is? Please don't tell me it's... No wait, it couldn't be those pricks with the razor paddle. They wouldn't go through all this effort. Who's driving the car?

41

I felt the car periodically stop, for signal lights probably. The car radio turned on and some girl with a smoker's voice started singing slowly to a lonely acoustic guitar. The car made turns and I rolled with them, getting different angles of the same soiled patch of cloth protecting my nuts from the elements. I tried to close my eyes, but couldn't.

I've really been through a lot the past few days. I know I'm losing weight cause my pants aren't fitting anymore and to make things worse what's left of my clothes have been shredded and stained beyond belief. I found a sport jacket a couple days ago and just put it on over my other clothes, but it didn't take long to turn that to shreds either. Even my shoes were falling apart. Expensive designer loafers reduced to leather moccasins. I didn't even want to think about my boxer shorts.

Can't smell myself, but I'm sure it's not pretty. I haven't washed in days and I've been sleeping in the streets, I've got to smell worse than diseased pig shit. And the crawling in garbage thing doesn't help. I'm starting to grow a beard and there's probably food from four days ago still in my mouth cause I haven't brushed my teeth. It probably smells like I've been eating shit.

Yup, I bet if anyone smelled me they'd either puke or pass out. I'd honestly say for the first time in my life I am disgusting. A grown man, with a once respectable job and family now walking the streets like some schizo. Things used to be so different. I used to be so different. I haven't wiped my ass in days.

The car hit a bump and I rolled over and fell in the puny foot well, at least now I didn't have my nose in my crotch.

I felt the compact slow down and finally stop. The driver shut off the engine and got out. I still had no control over the muscles in my limp body. But I felt the pain of my body smacking the concrete when I was dragged back out of the car.

For some reason, all fear left me and I was now just a curious lump of mass sitting in my skull waiting to see what happened next. I don't know if it was sheer lack of control, the fact that I am completely drained of energy or probably some combination of both. But I just don't have the energy to take hold of my body and fight back.

I had no choice but to let myself get awkwardly dragged through some parking structure, echoing with the yells of some domestic dispute, and into an elevator. Lying on my side on the elevator floor I could see a blurred reflection on the metal doors of my captor standing behind me. He was actually pretty short and dressed head to toe in dark clothes with a beanie covering half his head.

Then it was slide, slide on my back through the halls of some ratty hotel or apartment complex. I slid past one door after another till finally we entered one. The door shut leaving my captor and me in the darkness.

I lay on the floor breathing in the filthy dust of the carpet while I heard the other human in the room bumping into things and working their way around the room. Finally a switch was flicked and a dim light showed me I was either in the middle of some thrift store storage room or a teenager's bedroom. Stacks of used clothes surrounded every direction I could roll my eyes.

I could hear my captor walking around, he was breathing hard from dragging me, but I still couldn't see him. There was nothing I could do. I was still immobilized, paralyzed by fear.

He grabbed my ankles and wove my body between the piles. We knocked over a couple stacks but kept going. He dragged me backward into his bathroom and propped me up against the wall.

The guy turned the bathtub faucet on then started fiddling with the medicine cabinet with his back to me. I still hadn't had a good look at his face, but he had a small frame. If I had my strength, it would be nothing for me to take him out. I saw him set a bottle on the sink, then some gauze, another bottle and Band-Aids.

My nerves were almost shocked back to life when the body before me turned, and I saw with my two tired eyes 'he' was a 'she'. My mouth wanted to hang open and my eyes pop out, but my muscles wouldn't allow it. So I sat against the wall staring at this woman, no this girl, while she got ready to operate on me.

She left the room for a minute and came back carrying the largest pair of scissors you'd ever seen. She pushed me on my back and straddled me waving the scissors in my face, and for a second I thought she was going to cut my throat open. But instead she slipped the rusted blades under my collar and began cutting through the layers of clothes wrapped around my body. She cut away at everything till I was lying naked in all my reeking shame and hairy glory on her linoleum floor.

Then, without the slightest awkwardness on her part, she grabbed at my unshapely pale body and wrestled my limp limbs into the tub. Almost instantly the water turned gray then black and the bathroom began to smell like a sewer. How that girl kept from gagging I'll never know. And at once I felt tension starting to lift slowly. I still had no control over myself, but all fears I had before were gone completely now.

I laid in the shallow water of the tub staring at her from the corners of my eyes while she scrubbed five days worth of grime and humiliation from my body.

She was still wearing the black outfit with that beanie, and the contrast with her white skin made her look even whiter. She had a round little face that almost looked chubby, even though I could tell she must be thin under her clothes. Her lashes were long and made her dark brown eyes look seductive.

She wasn't bad looking, late twenties. But I had to admit she was attractive. Not the unshaven pervert I was expecting. She was reminding me of someone, but I kept forcing myself to ignore it.

When she started talking it was slow and soothing, almost hypnotic. "You're probably wondering a lot of things, yes?" She focused intently while she talked, never taking her eyes off my arms as she scrubbed them.

Hell yeah I'm wondering a lot of things! I wish I could squeeze the air out of my lungs and contort my lips to make words and sentences and ask her what the hell was going on. I also wanted to thank her, for what the hell was going on.

"Well my name is Sam. And as you can see I'm cleaning you up," she said in a sweet voice.

No shit.

"Well, where do I start, hmm," she said aloud. She seemed fully relaxed as she made circle motions on my back and stared off into space. "I guess the beginning. That place you went into tonight, the Black Spot, that's the name in case you didn't know. Well I used to work in there not too long ago. Maybe six months. Anyway the things they make us girls do in there, ugh!" she winced back at what must be a painful memory. I watched through the corner of my eye as she returned her focus back to the scrubbing. "Jesus, anyway, so us girls in there, let me just say we get worked bad. Real bad. The men they think they've got it all. They think

45

they're in control of it all," she said starting to scrub me hard, almost painfully.

"Oops I'm sorry," she lightened up her scrubbing. "I'm straying from the point. The point is."

Yes get to the point.

"The point is I worked in there and I know what goes on in there. And what the girls go through. And when those fucking assholes don't want the girls anymore. They take them to the alley out back, where you were, and they throw them out on the street. You know, it's like some kind of greyhound racing thing. When the dogs get too old to run, they get killed or let go. Same thing with us girls."

Okay, so you're an ex-employee. What does that have to do with me being here?

"So when it was time for me to get thrown out on the street, I went through shit for days. Getting fucking abused on the streets and scrambling to meet my needs. So I made a personal vow to help any girl that gets thrown out into that alley cause the bastard chauvinist pigs cant fucking make her bleed anymore." She was scrubbing me hard again, but caught herself again and eased up.

"So that's what I do, I sit up in the fire escape at nights waiting for the guards, bouncers, fucking assholes, whatever you want to call them, to bring out a poor girl. And after they leave her in the alley I come down and take her back her to my place," she said and I thought I caught a smile flash across her face.

"Here I can give her some fresh clothes."

I hope you aren't talking about the clothes in the entry. Those are anything but fresh.

"I can give her a good square meal," she continued. "Something you'll never see in that place. And I can get help get her on her feet."

You know, this girl is talking to herself. I'm looking at her from the corner of my eye, and her head is pointed in my direction, but she's staring off into God knows where. I bet she's thinking of something else behind those beautiful eyes. Those eyes, that's it!

I tried to forget about what I just thought. It was more than the eyes, it was the thin lips, the gaunt cheek bones, even the sharp bridge on her nose. The more I strained to look at her from the corner of my eyes, the more she looked like, like Christina. And the more I strained, the more the corners of my eyes burned and I wanted to close them.

I quit fighting the thoughts off and just let myself reminisce about Christina. Yes she had a striking resemblance to her. Yes, she reminded me of the way Christina would stare of into space when I'd try to have a serious conversation with her. Yes, that starry eyed, carefree looked really turned me on. Something my wife hasn't been able to do since nine months before the birth of our youngest.

The girl stopped brushing me for a second, took off her jacket leaving her in a tight tank top and then pulled the beanie off the top of her head letting a wave of long black hair fall around her shoulders.

Yes, I wish my fucking nerves to work so I could make a move on her and spend the night taking my frustration and passion out on her, just like Christina. I was salivating and mentally fucking her as hard as I could while she gently and innocently rinsed my back and started washing my hair.

"So tonight, just like all the others before, I crawled up the fire escape and waited for a girl to get dumped. I waited a long time, and about

47

halfway into it, I so those two jokers set you up and almost tear your face off like the other guy they got," she said.

And you didn't even try to help me, why?

"You're lucky you got into the Black Spot. Or should I say unlucky? Out of all the nights I've stalked that place, I've never seen anyone go in the back door before. I don't know how much so you saw in there-"

I saw enough.

"But you were in there a good while, while I waited outside and watched those jokers catch another fish. Then you, Paul and Joe burst out, looking like you got into some trouble and they beat the shit out of you, or should I say 'into'?" she snickered.

Har har, very funny. Keep rinsing my hair.

"Sorry I shouldn't have said that, but if you knew the stuff I've gone through, nevermind," she said seriously.

"So I waited around till the time the gig ends," she continued. "And no girls were taken out tonight and I don't like going home empty handed, so I grabbed you. Plus I felt really bad that you were suckered into going down that alley because you had good intentions. Anyway, now you're here."

What a girl.

"And don't you worry a thing. I'll get you fixed up just like all the girls that come this way. By the time you leave here, you'll be glad you went in there."

What a sweet, sweet girl. Mind if I call you Christina. You look just like her you know. God she was a good lay. I bet you're a good lay. I just wished I had my nerves back.

The girl finished up my bath silently. Then she drained the tub and rinsed me off with the shower hose. She had to dry me off in the empty tub and after a huge hassle of flopping arms and tangled legs, she got me back out of the tub. She gave up trying to get clothes on me and just wrapped an oversized robe around me then dragged me back out to the clothes littered living room.

"Alright, here you go," she said doing her best to shift me into a comfortable position on a dingy mattress in the corner of the room. "Oh wait I almost forgot."

She ran off to the bathroom and returned with a glass of water and a couple pills. She looked at me questioningly for a minute then broke the capsules open over the glass and let their powder dissolve turning the water a deep blue.

"Alright, we got to get you to swallow this," she said. "It'll help you heal faster."

Whatever you say, you're the nicest person I've met since I got here.

She gently tilted my head back and poured the mixture down my throat slowly. Amazingly my body had the muscle control to gag and cough up some of the liquid, but most of it made it down into my empty and aching belly.

"Alright, just go to sleep here and we'll get you fixed up in the morning." She winked at me and shut off the light and left me alone in the darkness. I listened as she stumbled her way out of the room and shut the door to what must have been her bedroom.

What a sweet girl. The world needs more people like her around. The new age Mother Teresa's.

All of a sudden it hit me like a freight train.

For the first time in days I felt my exhaustion catch up with me. I was so tired I couldn't think straight anymore. Everything became fuzzy, and my mind was working like a drunk. The warm bath, the massaging cleansing, the comfortable mattress, the sum of it all made my body start sinking into slumberland.

I kept thinking about my soft bed back home and the feeling of my wife's weight shifting around in the bed. Some people, they have problems sleeping. They say they can't sleep with noise, can't sleep with the heat or the cold. One thing that I have never had a problem with is sleeping. I have always been able to sleep. It doesn't even have to be a bed, I'll sleep on the cold floor of an emergency room. I don't care if there's a guy having heart recitation two feet away. Hell I could have a full nights rest if I was getting executed in the morning.

That's all I really need is sleep. And that's all I want right now, is to sleep. To lay here on this pile of musty clothes, breathing the cold damp air, close my eyes and sleep. I don't even need to count sheep I'm so tired. Just close my eyes. It'll happen soon. Just keep breathing and slipping further into the darkness behind my eyelids. I'll be gone in seconds. One. Two.

The last swirrly dirrly thought that sailed through my mind was an image of Christina playfully bouncing on a bed.

-THREE-

" You're as good as they get, and this is as good as it gets," I'd say to Christina time after time when we wrapped up another session. She pushed me off as joking around, but I was sincere. I really, honestly believed those words, at least during the times they were spilling out of my mouth, and no it wasn't just my penis talking.

Life was good and I was happy. It showed too, people could see the happiness overflowing in me and coming out in little laughs here and smiles there. I wasn't the same man that sat behind the desk all day massaging his temples and swallowing coffee faster than the machine could spit it out. I wasn't even the same husband and father who would drag himself through the front door every evening and collapse on the couch. I was an honest to God happy chum!

Things started changing in the most unforeseen ways. Rather than slacking off more at work cause I'd maybe spend good parts of an hour in Milton's unused office with the naked Christina Smith inventing new uses for office equipment, I'd actually become more productive and cheerful, spreading and boosting moral like a virus throughout the department. And instead of staying further away from my wife and kids because I was more interested in acting like a teenager after hours in a hotel room with a hot secretary, I actually ate dinner, at the table, with them, tucked the rascals in, for the first time, maybe ever, and stayed awake long enough to give my wife those back rubs she's always pinning for.

Yeah, you could say guilt was overshadowing me and I was doing everything I could to justify my actions in my head. Blaming it on my parents relationship, the TV shows I watched and natural instincts versus oppressive cultural restraint.

The new relationship was changing me, for the better. I was a new man, and the people I was around knew it too. Imagine, me of all people, actually having to think of an excuse to blame my newfound joy on. "Oh, it's just a new project at work that's got me all excited. It's my kid, he's uh, graduating from um, karate, yeah." Christina and I kept our affair secret, and we kept it damn good.

After a couple weeks they all just got used to it, the new me. Things were good. Life was good. Christina and I were good and the whole fucking solar system was aligned just for me and my prick.

But then she had to go and ruin it. Put a brick wall right in the way of my changed life.

Looking back on it now I wish I could somehow slip backwards through the seconds and slide my way behind months so I could go back in time and slap myself silly. I know the exact second I'd go back to. It was in the backseat of my family's station wagon and Christina Smith and I were half naked and giggling like a couple of retarded kids watching a Sunday cartoon. I was holding my dick mere millimeters away from her spread legs and trying to fight the alcohol so I could focus on getting it in. As a matter a fact I remember thinking to myself in a drunk sort of way how I better never regret this. And sure enough here I am regretting the whole idiotic childish thing.

That was the exact second I had permanently ruined my marriage with Melanie. Up until then I was innocent and free from anything the conniving Christina could have pulled out of her sleeve. But once I broke that fleshy seal and pushed my way into trouble it was irreversible.

No, you know what. I'd go back before that. Yeah, I'd go back to earlier that day before the whole bar and car thing and slap the shit of out of myself. And if I still didn't snap out of it, I knock myself out so I couldn't go through with it.

I had a huge fight with Melanie the evening before and spent the night on the couch with an empty stomach and a bottle of whiskey. Nothing unusual for us at that time. We averaged about two mild arguments a day and a couple major verbal fights per week. We'd had a good escalating track record of domestic disputes, non-violent of course, since we were forced to move into the apartment. But the difference this time could all be narrowed down to coincidences. Ah hell I can't fool myself, they weren't coincidences.

I'd love to say I was late for work cause I wasn't sleeping next to my alarm clock, and Christina just happened to be running late the very same day and time so we ran into each other at the entrance, and I'd even love to say it was mere coincidence that we decided to drown our troubles at the very same bar the very same evening and stumbled our way into the very backseat of the same car and even more amazingly we just happened to be naked and laying on each other. listening to the same song on the stereo. Damn, too bad it couldn't have been just that. What a coincidence!

But no, it had to be all opposites. I was too hung over to get up on time. And I was too lazy to take the longer, but faster route to work. And when I saw the sullen as usual looking Christina sitting behind her desk rolling a pencil under her finger tips and staring into the woodwork, I made my own two legs walk up to her desk and made my lips force a smile and speak the words which laid the foundation and got me into the shit hole.

And this is the moment I'd slap this shit out of myself and tell myself not to do it.

"Of course I know who you are. You pass my desk every morning and evening and I'm lucky if I get just a nod. But don't feel bad, that's all get from most of the people around here." When she said that last 'here', she snapped at a guy walking past her desk reading a paper. He didn't even glance at her.

"No one cares about the girl at the front who makes their copies and sorts their mail," she explained. "You know, it's just like this all over though. I've gotten used to it. I expect it now, so yeah. You're a surprise." All I asked was if she remembered me.

See was always saying too much. When just a yes or no would be sufficient, you'd get a lecture whatever she could think of at that second.

Probably why we could never sit and have a nice long talk, never. I always got frustrated cause I couldn't get a word in edge wise. As soon as my lips opened, she spit something from left field out.

"Yeah, so the guys must think I'm jailbait or something, and the girls, they got to be just jealous," she said still rolling the pencil and still staring into the empty desk in front of her.

"Jailbait?"

"Yeah, you know, under eighteen. Statutory rape, eighteen years of mashed potato dinner and a guys dick up your-"

I cut her off, "No, I know what jailbait means. Jesus! I just don't get why, why."

"Why what?" she said.

"Why anyone would think you're under eighteen."

"What I don't look it? You think I look old?" she asked looking at me for the first time with an accusing look.

This whole thing wasn't working out the way I thought. No, she didn't look eighteen, she looked thirty. I don't know what this girl was thinking. This wasn't going the way I wanted.

I stepped through those double doors five minutes ago sure as hell I was going to pick this girl up to get back at Melanie. You know, just take her out for dinner or something, nothing serious. Melanie had really worked me over last night. It was so bad I woke up nauseous with butterflies or whatever this morning. I wanted to get her back, I wanted to do something I knew would hurt her if she found out. I've taken Melanie's crap for the last time. I'm getting even and when I walked through those doors, I had a plan.

But this, this girl just destroyed it. I've said what, maybe two sentences and she's already freaking out on me or something. Forget it, it was a dumb idea anyway.

"Forget it," I said starting to walk away.

"Forget what?" she said. I was able to take a few steps and then she started talking again. "Wait."

"Wait, what?" I said stopping.

We looked at each other with dumb faces for a second.

"Well, forget what?"

"I was going," I was thinking about making something up on the spot instead of asking her out. But then I remembered Melanie and her stupid arguments about the dumbest things. And how if I let this slip by I'd just go home like everyday before this one. And deal with the same crap as yesterday. And then I'd be sleeping on the couch drunk all over again and-. "Dinner?" I cut myself off.

"Dinner?" she looked at me questioningly, and then she understood. "Oh, um," she hesitated for a second. I really didn't care if she rejected me. It was that point in my life where I wasn't caring too much about anything. If my food order was messed up, if I missed my TV show, where my daughter was after school, if that mole on my neck was cancerous or even if I was crushed by a semi crossing the street. Lately I, just, don't, care.

"Sure."

"What? Are you serious?" I wasn't really shocked at her answer. I was more shocked at what I had just done.

I'm a thirty-four year old man with a wife and two kids at home. One's just a toddler, but the other's old enough to know what daddy spending too much time with Mrs. Rhodes means. I'm the guy next door pushing the old mower around on Saturday. I'm supposed to be the happy father carving the turkey on Thanksgiving and flipping burgers on the Fourth, surrounded by smiling relatives. Yeah, I've got a stack of dirty mags tugged away in the attic, but I'm not a cheater. I'm no wandering dog looking for pussies. I love my wife. I love my family. I just, damn. I'm just in rut that's all. No, that's not true about loving my family, now I'm just lying. The truth is, I *want* to love my family. I did, I used to. But that feeling's not there anymore. I guess it just burned out?

Alright. Look, as far as it goes with Melanie and me, we did everything by the book. Everything, and it still turned out rotten. We dated for a couple years and lived together before saying the I do's. We were great together. Our lives consisted of going out late weekend nights, afternoon sex, sleeping in and just plain doing whatever we wanted, oh and no money worries. It was a true honeymoon period. Even my close friends were telling me the same thing. "Don't get used to it buddy. It's not going to last, it's the honeymoon phase." And of course I had to disagree, and tell them Melanie I were different. We had something. Or at a least that's what I wanted to believe.

But sure enough, things started changing. Our first born came around and there went half the freedoms. No more going out late weekend nights. No more spontaneous mini vacations. There was a new body in the house and it needed more attention than a chemist could give studying his experiments. The first fracture had come between Melanie and me.

But we managed, and things lightened up as our daughter grew. After a while we hired babysitters so we could start going out again. Full nights of sleep came back and our sex life was repaired here and there, but it was never the same. All in all it was still a comfortable life in the suburbs for the next few years. Until the birth of our second.

Bradly, was, well we thought he was just different at first. You know, maybe a little slower with the talking thing than most kids, but still normal. But on his second birthday while everyone's all distracted with getting the big cake and candles ready, the kid crawls off into a closet and it takes us a good half hour to find him. Thank God I was the first to see him, Melanie would have lost it for sure. Baby Bradly was laying on his side next to our German Shepard getting his birthday present a little too early. The kid was literally suckling on our dog like some puppy. After that we kept an eye on his behavior closely, and sure enough a month later he's taken his birthday blocks and lined them all up nice and neat down the hall. But that's not it, over the next few days he lines up everything he can get his hands on cups, empty cans, shoes all in perfectly straight lines down the hall that would make even a mason jealous.

Bradly was diagnosed with autism. The mild fracture between Melanie and me deepens.

Melanie quits her job to focus on Brad. A fissure forms.

I work overtime to make up for the pay. This doesn't look good, the crack gets worse.

We're forced to sell the house and move into an apartment. Melanie and I are near splitting.

The fissure grew into a wide crack, then a gashing fault till finally one last chip and Melanie and my relationship broke us apart completely. Emotionally we were two entirely different people now. All the shit took a toll on our relationship till finally I got sick just being in the same room with her. Sleeping in the same bed, ha! That was a joke. The only thing that joined us, besides the roof over our head, was the flimsy little piece of printed paper called a marriage license.

When we were first going out and into the marriage, Melanie was my angel. She wasn't the best looking girl in the room, but she was mine and I was proud. She used to laugh at everything and had a talent of being able to make the most boring situation funny and interesting. It was that goof ball, easy going quality that attracted me to her. But the kids, and the finance trouble, it all took a toll on her. That funny side faded and what was left was a sour, tired woman. And I had to come home to this bitter woman every evening, sleep next to the prude every night, and wake up to her banging stuff around in the kitchen every morning. The Melanie I married no longer existed. I was now married to the wicked witch of the bedroom. Emotionally she was cold and the colder she got, the colder I got.

And then the arguments sank in. Oh God the arguments. It would start off real logical having a point, an objective. A perfectly structured arguments fit for professional debates room across the country and then somewhere between A and B the whole damn thing would fall apart and we'd be yelling about the Goddamn bathroom towels. Everything we yelled about the smart things. Money, kids, property, our future finance and we'd yell even louder about the pointless things, pets, towels, toilets, boxes, washing your hands, snoring. The Goddamn thing was a fucking mess that would go hours into the night and span days, weeks. One time we didn't sleep together for a whole fucking month just because of something I cant even remember now.

So much yelling just turned our house in a ridiculous court t.v. talk show. Ladies and gentlemen please witness party X yell loudly about dishes and childcare and witness party Y yell even louder about rent and electricity. Jury place your verdict, both guilty. Both guilty for the crime of noise pollution and mind corruption, pollution. I sentence both of you to restless nights and heavy guilt with 20 years of ever escalating blood pressure. But there is a way out, all you have to do is shut up!

Melanie and I had officially entered divorce territory, but neither of us wanted to say it. I was just too exhausted to do much of anything. Day and night I dragged myself around trying to get the simplest things done. And Melanie, well I think she just couldn't bear what would happen to Brad if we separated.

Then came the episodes of neglect. It was always I've got to go here and there and everywhere. She was never home. If she was, it was either in front of the t.v. or asleep. Or asleep in front of the t.v. The woman wouldn't give me the time of day or rarely sit the same room as me. The silent treatment would go on for days at a time. After a while I got used to it. Just kind of started ignoring her as well. We just disappeared from each others lives like the other had died without a funeral.

So we put up with it, each other that is. We avoided each other as much as possible. If we ever did cross paths, it was a certain disaster. And things went this way for three years.

Three very long years.

Years of working my ass off while she sits around making Spaghetti O's and cleaning up drool. Years of paying the bills while she pines about never having enough to do the things she wants. Years of burning my brain and body out and having her yell about how I never want to do anything any more.

I was on the edge, and all it took was that one last argument to push me off. So when I say I wanted to get Melanie back, and when I say I wanted to feel human again, you can just imagine how much I wanted to take a girl out. There's nothing wrong with that, right? Completely innocent, strictly platonic. Something simple, coffee. Maybe dinner, but that's it. I just want to feel positive human emotions again.

I chose Christina to be that girl in the car on the way to work. I just put on one of my old tapes in the car stereo and got myself all pumped up to ask her out. Every time I felt cold feet coming on, I turned the music up louder. By the time I pulled into the parking lot the volume knob was as high as it could get and my ears were ringing. I was doing this. I needed to do this. I had to do this.

Like I said, I'm just in a rut. That's all. Give me some time and I'll pull out.

I'm not going to sleep with Christina. I'd never cheat on Melanie for the sake of making things worse. I won't even kiss Christina. At most dinner and that's it.

I repeated those words in my head all day and even while I was walking up to the restaurant I was meeting Christina at.

"Hey!" Christina said running up behind me.

I turned around and saw her trying to catch her breath and finish clipping her hair back while talking about some dog or something.

"I'm sorry I'm late," she panted, "but I forgot I had my dog at the groomers and they won't hold him overnight so I had to pick him up, and he messed my outfit up cause I had to hold him in my lap while I drove home, so I had to re-change and that took more time but I raced over as fast as I could." All in one breath. "Hey wait, why are you late?"

"Um, I'm not," I said too serious for her to recognize it was a joke. So she just stared at me. "I'm just kidding," I tried to smile.

I thought going out with Christina, or any girl really, would make me feel better about myself, but so far all I was getting was butterflies and paranoia that I was going to run into someone that knew Melanie and me.

"Haha, very funny Mister," she said unimpressed. "Why were you really late?"

"I, I don't know. Traffic I guess," damn was I good at lying. Who cares anyway? I didn't tell her the truth was cause I had stopped off in a gas station parking lot for twenty minutes to think about what I was doing with my life. I finally had to pop in another one of my old rock tapes to get the courage to finish the drive to the restaurant.

She gave me a silent 'what the hell is he thinking' stare. "Whatever, let's go get something to eat." She said hurrying us to the door.

So I showed up, barely, at least I came at all.

Dinner was whatever. I was quiet most of time and let Christina jab her head off. I wasn't paying too much attention. Most of the time my mind was fantasizing about what Melanie would think if she found out about this and I was debating whether her reaction would be jealousy, or a filing for divorce the next morning. Should I really care? It was weird, during this meal I was actually feeling something emotional. I actually wanted Melanie jealous.

However there were moments I was able to squeeze Christina into my mind. Usually when she'd make some comment she thought was the funniest thing ever said and she get herself started on a laughing roll. Christina had that quirkiness, that fun energy Melanie used to have. There were times I'd close my eyes and look away and just imagine she was the old Melanie.

When I'd open my eyes and look across the table, there was Christina. In her own little world poking at her plate and muttering something. She really was attractive. I feel bad saying it, but much more attractive than Melanie. She was thinner all over, even her face was a little gaunt but in a good way, a striking sleek and sexy way. Like a young Courtney Cox. Her face had real character. She had light skin but it only helped make her dark brown eyes stand out more. And her straight hair fell perfectly around her shoulders. I hate Melanie's short curls, they look greasy. This girl was the old Melanie and more.

The dinner wasn't all bland and me thinking away in my head. Christina managed to get a couple laughs out of me when she spilled water on her top then got sauce on her arm while reaching for the napkin. She laughed too, so I'm glad she didn't take it as an insult. We were even able to start up a conversation about her dog and then why people have pets in the first place. But it died when she got distracted trying to get the waiter to bring us free dessert.

After dinner she talked me into taking her out for a drink. To tell you the truth I didn't want to go. I'd gotten what I wanted already, a night out away from Melanie with a beautiful woman. But it wasn't making me feel the way I wanted. I thought I'd get some rejuvenating feeling or something. I don't know, maybe I just can't feel that way anymore. You know that lust for life, fresh and anticipating feeling you have when you're young. Instead all I was getting from this was paranoia and anxiety, exhaustion. The only reason I took Christina up on her drink offer was cause she said she'd pay and I could choose the place, plus I wanted to give that rejuvenation feeling one more go.

I wanted to take separate cars but she forced me into driving her. So I started us off toward a little place called The Wheel, but when Christina saw it was just a coffee house she swore she wouldn't leave the car unless we went to this bar she knows. The Wheel was the coffee house Melanie and I used to go sometimes on a weekend night after a movie or something. Looking back on it now, I wish I wouldn't have listened to her. You hear that Christina, screw your bar and your little girl games.

The bar was what I expected. On the outskirts of town and the kind of place where you could find a fistfight in the parking lot on any given Saturday night. Walking through the door I expected to find half a dozen guys slouched over the bar belching away, but the place was pretty bare. There were a couple guys watching a sport game at the bar and that was about it. Maybe 10pm was early over here?

Anyway, Christina got us a round of cheep drinks from the bar and we sank into a table in the darkest corner.

I still couldn't get over the fact that I was out with this woman. Not only was this something I would have never had the balls to do before, but this woman was gorgeous. Not in the movie star cover of glossy magazines way, but probably more in the approaching middle age guy who hasn't been alone with a woman in way too long is having too much too drink and would think any woman was super attractive way. She was simple, plain, but beautiful. I wanted to sneak peaks at her legs.

So we sat in our corner, trying to ignore everything around us and doing almost the exact same thing we were doing in the restaurant. Which was pretty much Christina doing the talking and me doing the staring and nodding. For every word I said, she said ten. She started off talking about interests, schools, silly family stories, then shifted to her personal problems. Ex-boyfriends, abusive relationships, money trouble. Great.

For the past twenty minutes I've been sitting here alternating my stare between Christina and the floor. Christina, floor, Christina floor. I can't believe I'm actually doing this, Jesus Christ we barely met this morning. She's pouring drinks down her throat and telling me about all this fucked up shit in her life while I just keep on staring and thinking. Her endless chatter is getting old and I'm pretty sure my stale stare is too. I'm getting anxious to end it now. This whole thing seems so pointless to me. Why am I here again?

"Yeah, so my dad left my mom when I was only eight. I think, maybe I was nine? Does it really matter? Anyway the chauvinist left her for another woman. Can you believe that?" she said buzzed. She stopped to take a gulp of her drink. It was a Long Island now, but five minutes ago it was dark beer, she was working her way up.

Since she brought up the whole cheating stuff I started feeling nauseas. I was already over this whole thing and just wanted to get back home. What the hell was I thinking? Look at me I'm thirty-three with a wife and two kids at home. I'm not some young hormone infected guy who does this stuff. I'm past the whole going out to bars and picking up girls phase. That was a decade ago for me. I just want to get home watch some TV, eat some dinner and get to bed. It's been a long day.

"I guess I wine about the bastard a lot but I don't really give a shit," she said. She downed half the Long Island without making a face. I'm going to assume it was a weak pour. Then she leaned across the table and looked me deep in the eyes. "But you want to know something that's even more fucked up?"

65

I guess I was supposed to answer her, but I just stared at her, then let my eyes fall back to the floor.

"Well, I'm going to tell you. Even if my dad was a prick who couldn't live with his mistake. I, and you wont believe this, I support what he did," she paused and stared straight at me as if expecting me to gasp or something. I didn't budge, I just stared back and wondered how much longer this whole thing was going to go on. "Yeah. I agree with the pig. I totally understand why he left us. And if I were him I would have left us too. You know why?"

This girl was seriously talking to a wall. I wasn't shocked, I wasn't curious I really didn't give a shit about her messed up childhood and cheating dad or anything. I'm at the point where I'm waiting for a good point in her little monologue so I can break in and try and end this conversation and night. Maybe if I tell her I've got a meeting in the morning, naw too lame and cliché.

"Because she was a bitch. A mother fucking bitch that I grew to hate more and more every day. I have never met anyone in my life that I hated more than my mom. Go ahead tell me I'm a little brat, I'm arrogant or whatever you want. But it's the truth. My mother was a genuine bitch from hell."

Ok, I've got it! I excuse myself for the restroom when the times right, like in a couple seconds. Then I come back and tell her I'm not feeling well and gotta get home. It's kinda embarrassing, but after what this girl's told me I don't think she'll care.

"I don't know it was like she was trapped in her adolescence or something. She was always competing with me and it just got worse as I got older. At first it was like she was trying to be my best friend. Keeping me home from school some days so we could go to the mall and shop together. She'd even smoke out with me sometimes. How's that for mother daughter quality time. Yeah, that was whatever. Some people call it cute, I call it lame. But then when I got to high school and started ditching school with my own friends and smoking dope with them, she entered jealousy stage. I wasn't her little sister, or best friend anymore. I was now the popular girl at school she envied and hated. She did everything she could to fuck me up. She messed with my school homework, stole the money I made from my shitty job, told my friends embarrassing shit about me. She even tried to screw my boyfriends!"

That last line caught my attention and I snapped my head up from staring at the ground. I think she could tell cause she stopped talking and just stared at me with this look on her face. I couldn't tell if it was anger or curiosity but whatever. She downed the rest of her Long Island and didn't take her eyes off me the whole time.

There was about thirty seconds of silence. Me staring at the floor and I could see from the corner of my eye she was staring at me. "Listen, I've got to-"

I was going to tell her I had to go to the bathroom then come back and pull off the master plan. But she cut me off and ruined things, again.

"You think you're cool huh."

What? "What?" I thought, then said. What?

"Look at you Mr. Big man at the office. Picking up the secretary and taking her out to a bar. Look at you just sitting there staring off into space like you're the only thing that matters. You think you're all slick and everything cause you're going out with a girl half your age, huh."

"Half my age?" that was an insult. "I'm only 33! Missey."

67

She tilted her head and looked at me then kinda laughed. "I guess it's the lighting, you look a lot older. Are you sure?"

"Sure what? About my age. Jesus." I don't know why but this girl just pushed my button. "I've had a rough 24 hours alright. Things haven't exactly been swell."

She stopped mocking me and talked serious for a second, "oh a rough 24 hours, eh. Fuck man. My past 22 years of life haven't been swell."

"Yeah, well it's been a while for me too," I started but then thought, what the hell do I want to tell this stupid 22 year old. She'll never understand half the things I've gone through. "You know what, forget it. Life's fucked up. We can both agree about that. Let's go."

"What, no, no siree. You can't do that to me," she said. "We're not leaving. Stay right here I'll be right back."

"No really, I've got to get going its getting late."

She looked at me and laughed, "What are you joking, getting late? This coming from Mr. Slick who's only 33. I'll be right back."

I just sat there like a corpse and watched her walk to the bar where it looked like she was picking up more drinks. Dammit I want to go, I don't want to spend all night drinking and listening to some dumb woman whine to me about this and that and life. Actually as bad as it sounds, that's what I do every night.

She came back and practically threw the drink at me. "What's this?" I asked taking a sip. Jesus! It was like drinking straight alcohol. 200 proof, fire water.

"Just drink it, Mr. Slick," she said then took a nice drink from whatever she had. "Now I just got through telling you how my mother fucked one of my boyfriends, so you better not hold back about your life. I want to hear what could make you think your life isn't *swell*."

"I thought you said your mom tried to have sex with your boyfriend, not did?"

"Forget about that bitch and quit stalling," she said.

Why do I feel like I'm out with a teenager?

I took a long drink and waited for the burning feeling to leave my throat. I really didn't want to be here, but she bought me a drink already. It tastes like shit, but I cant complain its free alcohol and my brain has been living off alcohol lately. Besides if I went home I'd just be doing the same in a different place with a different woman, only it would be worse cause there'd be yelling and throwing and cussing and kids crying, oh Jesus. I took another gulp.

Alright, just tell her your story, you don't have to say everything. Just enough to get you through the drink then you'll call it a night and leave. I looked across the table and saw Christina was already half done with her drink. Man, she doesn't waste any time.

"Oh, where to begin," I sighed and looked off. I felt the warmth of alcohol growing in my stomach, man this stuff is quick.

"Start at the beginning, when you first fell into this world. Was your dad there in the delivery room or off doing it with another woman?" she butt in.

"I don't know. I mean I don't know if he was there or not, but I know he wasn't with another woman. Look, my childhood wasn't like that. I have to admit it was pretty good," I said. "I grew up in another small town around here and made it all the way to my mid 20s without getting into too much trouble."

69

Christina leaned back in her chair and smirked at me, "what happened then?"

"Then, I got married."

Shit! I didn't mean to say that! I got distracted and comfortable feeling alcohol's warmth and let it slip. Crap any second now she's going to jump up and slap me. Alright, brace yourself. You know what, who cares. If she slaps me, it just means I get home sooner.

She just sat there.

"Ok, go on," she said. "Why'd you stop?"

"Huh? Aren't you," I didn't know what to say and she could tell.

"Then you got married," she said trying to help me remember what I had just said.

"No, I know what I said. I just thought you'd," I started.

"I'd what? Be shocked," she said. "Oh sorry. Let me try that again." She stared at me with half a smile and eager eyes. "Well?"

"Well what?" I asked.

"Well say it again."

"What?" I asked. What was this girl talking about was she smoking something?

"Say you're married retard," she said still looking eager.

"I'm married?" I half said, half asked.

"What!" her face exploded into exaggerated shock and she threw her arms in the air. "You're married oh my God! You never told me!" She was kind of yelling and I noticed the few guys at the bar turn around to glance at us for a second. "Holy shit! I mean I saw the ring on you're left index finger and all, but crap I never thought it mean't you were, you know, married" she was trying hard not to laugh at herself, again. "No, no and don't tell me that woman and those two kids in the picture in your wallet are your family!" She closed her eyes and put her hand up to forehead then let her head fall forward on the table almost knocking the glasses over

I didn't know what to think. And I pretty much didn't get a chance because she started laughing at her little drama queen scene then started talking again.

"Well, Mr. Slick was that better?" she asked picking her head up. "Was I shocked enough for you?"

I was speechless, what the hell was going on? I haven't been drinking that much to be imagining things even though my body was tingling. Damn, I am retarded. The ring was obvious and she must have caught a glance at the pictures when I opened my wallet at the restaurant.

"Why are you the shocked looking one?" she said slowing her laugh. "Oh wait, I get it! Oh my God!" She looked at me and then covered her mouth and started laughing again. "I get it. I get it," she repeated. "You've never done this before have you?" she said looking like she just found the holy grail.

She had to wait a little while for me to get over my confusion and answer her. And all she got out of my mouth was a little whimper, "What?"

"You never done this, huh. This whole cheating thing."

"Cheating? I'm not cheating!" I snapped back to alert and got all defensive. "I'm not cheating."

"Hey, hey Mr. Slick. Alright you're not cheating. You're just out with a young girl at a bar and your wife has no clue about it," she said with a smirk on her face. She was obviously not taking this serious at all.

"That's not cheating," I said getting red in the face, and it wasn't cause of the booze.

"Then what is it?"

I don't know why, but she didn't react the way I thought she would to the married thing. I guess with all the other fucked up signs she'd been giving me I should have expected it. Instead of jumping up and slapping me, which I kinda wanted so I could get home, she just nodded and took another drink.

"Look, I've had enough it's time to go," I've really had enough and I started to push my chair out to get up.

She didn't move but as soon as I was almost standing she started talking real fast. "No wait," she said. "I don't care. Honestly."

"It's not you I care about," I said. I didn't care about my wife and marriage either though. "Let's go."

"Wait please," she said sounding panicky. It looked like she was sobering up and losing that giddy girl face. "Alright it's not cheating I'm sorry I said it."

Why is she so intent on staying? "It's not the cheating thing! Will you stop talking about it. Let's just go."

"Then what is it? Tell me, I'm sorry," she said seriously.

"Yeah, what is it?" some guy from the bar yelled.

"Haha, answer the lady," another drunk voice shouted.

I looked up and saw all the guys at the bar had their backs to the game on TV and were watching us. One guy looked at me and raised his beer like he was congratulating me, then took a swig. The others just laughed and one guy looked like he was starting to choke on his pretzels or something and his buddy slapped his back. Oh God this place was trashy. Christina gave them the finger.

I returned to Christina and gave her a cold stare, "What do you care?" It was mean I know it. She didn't really do anything to cause the shit I was going through. She'd really been actually kinda nice all night. Let's face it, the marriage comment could have ended a lot worse. I guess I just turned into a dick on her real fast cause she was the person in front of me at the moment. It could have been Mother Teresa and I'd still tell her off. Of course the alcohol probably had something to with it. For some reason whenever I drink it always brings out the emotions inside of me at the moment. It's like a truth serum. I swear if you get me drunk, or even buzzed, and I'm in the right mood you can get all kinds of information out of me. I just feel bad Christina had to see this side of me right now. The angry, frustrated me. Sorry Christina. "Let's go," I said in a softer voice.

She didn't say a word and just stood up and followed me. "Wait," she said and finished her drink off in a gulp then grabbed my unfinished one and took it with her. "I paid good money for this, we can't waste it."

I led us out of the trashy bar vowing I'd never come back, never even drive past this place again. Little did I know, I'd be back here again in a week with Christina, only without all the gloom and anger surrounding me.

We walked silently to my car and I opened the door for her, just to be nice. She said thank you. I felt a little better now that we were out of there and I could see the end of the evening nearing.

I got in on my side and stuck the key in to start the engine.

"Before you start the car," she said. It was too late though I had already turned the engine. Christina stuck her arm out and turned the key, stopping the engine. Alright I guess it wasn't too late. "I want you to tell me something."

"What?"

"Here drink this first," she held out the half finished drink she bought for me. "Then tell me what's going on in your head."

"No thanks, I'm not drinking that," I tried to politely refuse.

"What? I buy you the drink, smuggle it out here, all for you. And you still refuse?" she said, but in a soft voice. Almost sweet like. I looked at her and she gave me a little smile.

"I don't know what that is and I'm already pretty buzzed. That'll probably put me over the edge."

Without taking her eyes of mine, she unraveled my fist and wrapped my palm and fingers around the cold glass. That was the first time she touched me and it struck me how soft and delicate she was. That night I remember going over the whole evening again and again in my head and analyzing every second. I remember thinking about that hand moment the most. Trying to relive it and look at it like symbolism. Like she was gently breaking down my walls and opening me up, she was telling me not to be afraid, that she was there and would help guide me. I thought she was my angel.

It wasn't until the end of the relationship did I think back to that moment and look at it a little closer. Just close enough to see what she was really doing. She wasn't just opening me up, but she was also putting something in that hand. And it wasn't love and warmth. It was an ice cold, hard object filled with poison. And that's the truth. She was opening me up and invading me and my life with her evil self. Christina was no angel. She was deceiving, like the devil or a republican.

But at the time I was confused and vulnerable. So I fell for it. I accepted the glass and filled my stomach with the burning toxin.

I don't know if it was like a therapy session or what, but I guess the cold night, Christina holding my hand, the alcohol, my overflowing emotions; it all came together and opened me up. Just like Christina wanted. I just kept talking and she just kept listening and holding my hand. She left the car for a minute and came back with more drinks. So I went back to my talking and she kept feeding me more drinks. Till finally the poison mixed with the my blood in my veins and I was completely drunk.

I told her just about everything that I'd been holding in. I told her about my failing marriage. What our marriage and Melanie turned into, our first kid the bratty daughter, my disabled boy with the dog. And we were laughing our asses off and I know if I was sober I'd be feeling real ashamed but something was going on in me and I was letting go.

For the first time in too long, I was letting go of it all and just doing and saying what I wanted. Year's worth of shit and emotions tucked away in the back of my mind just came spewing out of my mouth. I know I wasn't speaking right. My sentences were probably choppy and incomplete but I just kept going. I wasn't talking to tell Christina my problems anymore, I was talking to tell *me* my problems. And as long I understood what was flooding out of my mind and mouth I was getting somewhere.

I was laughing and crying at the same time. I went through pretty much the entire range of emotions in a few minutes. Happiness, confusion, depression, anger and regret and the whole blabbering clumsy thing ended in laughter. I wasn't making sense on the inside anymore either. One second I was thinking about my messed up life and the next I was thinking about the guys back at the bar. I want to go back and kick their asses but I can't stay focused. Everything in my head just turned upside down and jumped from topic to topic faster than a kid with ADD. I'm trying to think clearly, but I can't the alcohol is stopping me. I must think clear, I must think so I can, so can. Why do I want to think clear again? Why? Shit I'm wasted, I'm not going to think clear. I give up.

Who knows what Christina's thinking? Who cares? She's laughing, and I'm laughing. She just said something about pretzels and choking and now she's laughing harder. I guess we're both drunk then, aye Christina? A couple of drunks in the old station wagon that I try to make look clean and new but it doesn't, cause a station wagon can never look clean and new. I laugh. I've got to kick the shit out of those guys. But just one more drink first. I try to grab one of the glasses Christina lined up on the dash but I spill the liquid colors on my arm. Haha, Christina try's to lick it off, but I'm moving around too much. Man she has a long tongue.

I'm done with my problems and my life. I want to think about Christina and her looks, her body. That sexy body in the seat next to me. I'm trying to focus on moving my lips so I can tell her she's prettier than my wife and has bigger tits. I told you booze makes me honest, and did I mention vulgar? She's laughing and I'm pushing it. I throw some more flirty comments at her and her body, I don't know if the words actually came out though. My lips aren't working too good.

And she's punching my arm and I'm punching back. Is this sexual harassment? Did she flash me a shot down her shirt? My mind isn't processing normal, I mean right, right now. Haha, right? God is she hot.

Was she this sexy before? The windows are fogging up but I don't care I'm staring at her skirt and thighs. She puts her hand on my face to block my view, so I open my mouth and suck one of her fingers. She laughs and yanks her hand away.

Ok I know I didn't imagine her hand on my leg just now. Should I do it? Should I take a chance and grab her?

Too late, I've got my hand on her thigh right now and she's just laughing and acting like it's not even there. Holy shit! I'm getting fresh with this hot girl. Look at me now Melanie! Now who's the boring one? The one who doesn't want to go out anymore and have fun. Man I'm having fun!

I took it a step a further and ran my hand halfway up her skirt and she went with it. Christina just squealed and grabbed me between the legs.

My mind is blacking out for seconds at a time now. I'm seeing the world in flashes. One flash and she's leaning forward to kiss me and the next flash I've got my mouth on her neck and her hair is all over my face. There are more flashes of Christina laughing and the car doors and the next thing I know we're somehow in the back seat and Christina's already got her shirt off. I grab at my shirt to catch up and realize mine is already gone. So are my pants. Jesus!

Alright this flash is important. Try and gain control. FIGHT THE ALCOHOL! Try and focus. My arms aren't working right. Don't black out again. One, two, three. Think. Focus. Christina's laying on her back with her panties off and her skirt up. I'm naked between her legs. It looks like I'm all ready to go. Just another inch and I'm in. Do I want this? Think, think, focus. Will people regret this? I mean will I regret

77

anything? Isn't the world full of regret or how does that saying work? You'll never regret what you don't do? What the fuck am I thinking? Screw it, exactly!

Screw the world! Screw it all! Fuck, fuck, fuck you Melanie! Fuck me! Screw this pussy!

All the emotions in the world were driving my hips. One for my depressing marriage, two for my frustrating underpaid job, three for the disgusting apartment, four cause I'm pissed at myself for never doing anything about anything, five for the happiness I only feel when I'm drunk. Six for, six, six? Sex! I pounded the shit out of Christina and listened to her scream about it.

I don't know how long it lasted but that moment of my life I spent looking through my eyes at one horny flash after another and listening to my mind yell at everything that I had issues with and more. It was lust and cyclothymic emotions at their best. I don't know how else to explain it, except that for God knows how long I went through some kind of twisted carnal-self-psychoanalysis in the back seat of the old station wagon.

It ended with me blowing all my frustration, problems and shit out all over her stomach.

Juices, emotions and sweat got everywhere.

I have never felt so relieved in my life.

So, so alive.

So, human.

And that's pretty much how the relationship worked. I never grew or bonded with Christina intellectually or emotionally, I just used her to release my inner turmoil and stress. The same way people with free time get rid of stress by exercising or meditation or an old person with a hobby. And don't people use their pets that way too? In the past Christina and I tried marriage counselors. They only made things worse. I tried a shrink, but he charged too much and never gave me answers. Finally Christina comes along, and for once something works. Sex. The greatest stress reliever and rejuvenation life could prescribe. Sex with a new, hot little something.

I hadn't had such a good time in years. I was beginning to think I had forgotten how to laugh and fuck. Even how to be human. Think those happy thoughts and such. I'd thought I'd given up my best years to Melanie. Even the kids brought misery instead of joy. I thought I was through feeling anything but shit. Then Christina came along.

It was too much to take at first, like being handed someone else's life. Hormones I forgot existed pulsed through my mind, and I couldn't stay mad for more than a minute before thoughts of Christina's body came in and cleaned house. A hardon stiff as a teenager's. I'd get this stupid grin on my face, honestly. A full grown man, smiling at nothing and having to shun inquisitions about why he'd stare off smiling at nothing in the middle of dinner.

Everyday for a straight month I was that old fashioned black and white character dancing down the streets smelling the roses and swinging on the light posts. I couldn't wait till the next moment I could get Christina naked and slide between those beautiful cellulite-free legs.

For once I have an outlet. For once I leave and come home with a smile on my face. For once I am the father and husband everyone wanted. For once I have a secret so big if it got out, lives would be permanently ruined.

Christina never knew what I was using her for. Because of this, I thought I was on top, I was in control. But I wasn't. I told you Christina was deceiving, and I told myself I thought it was weird the way she was so eager with me the day we met. One day she told me something she had managed to keep hidden from me the whole time.

We were laying in bed at our regular hotel after my 'therapy' session and she said:

"Remember how you lied to me?"

"Lied about what?" I asked. I was laying on my back completely relaxed.

"About your marriage," she said.

"What do you mean?"

"Well, you never told me you were married when you picked me up at the office on our first date," she said. "Remember, it was only about a month ago?"

"I guess, what's your point?" I was starting to get a little curious. Christina was never talkative like this after we had sex, so something was up.

"Well remember how I reacted when you told me you were married?"

"Yeah," I remembered alright but I didn't want to. I never really liked recalling our moments that night before the hand thing in the car. It brought back horrible feelings in me. The new me is optimistic and positive, not depressed and frustrated.

"Well I've got a secret too," she said slowly while she slipped her hand between my legs.

I'm sure it's nothing. I can handle anything now, at work or at home.

I'm the suburban superman.

She waited till I was hard again before saying, "I've got a kid."

Kryptonite! I didn't budge and she kept rubbing. I froze in my head, what does this mean? Is this bad? Horrible feelings are coming back and superman is disintegrating. Ok, think this out don't just go nuts. Ok, Christina has a kid. So what? A lot of people have kids. They're nice, at least when they have the right chromosomes. Even then Bobby is nice.

"Kids are great," I said aloud.

"If you can afford them," she said.

We laid there in silence for a while. My junk turned to putty. I kept imagining what she was thinking. What kind of thing is that to say, if you can afford them? Should I ask her what she means by that? No, no don't say a word. Just lay here as if she didn't say anything at all. Maybe I can forget this little conversation.

Christina got on top of me and started kissing my face. I felt my stomach turn. I let her kiss me but I didn't kiss back.

I think she got the hint cause she stopped and just laid on me like a dead body.

"I need something," she whispered.

A dead body that talks. I felt my stomach get heavier. I didn't say a word.

"I've got some bills," the dead body said. "Big ones."

Ok, just don't say anything. A lot of people have big bills. I know what she's thinking but I'm not going to say anything, yet.

We just laid there, listening to our breathing. This is one of the slowest conversations I have ever had. I wish we hadn't done this today, I'm starting to feel really sick.

"So will you help me?"

Don't get mad, don't start yelling. This isn't bad. Just tell her the truth, "I can't."

"Why not?" her soft tone of voice was gone.

"Cause I can't afford it."

"What do you mean you can't afford it?"

Just like one of the conversations I used to have with my wife.

"I can barely afford my own bills."

"Come on, you're practically the manager. I know you've got money."

"It doesn't pay as much as you think. And remember my wife has no job and I've got the two kids, one with autism," I said. See I was handling this pretty well. "You know I'd help you if I could."

She rolled off me and laid quietly for a little while. Ok, I've got to leave. This is just bringing me down. I started to roll my legs off the bed.

"You have to give me money," she said.

I sat up, "Look, Christina. I don't want to talk about this now or again. So I'm just going to say it once." I sat on the edge of the bed with my back to her body. "I barely make enough money to make ends meet at home. So I definitely don't make enough money to help pay for your bills," they were cold words and I sounded like a robot but I really didn't have a choice. "In the future, if I get promoted, then maybe I will have enough money to help. But until then please don't ask."

Damn did all that just come out of my mouth? I think I was just as shocked as Christina, assuming she is. Wow. Suburb superman is back!

"If you don't give it to me, the court will make you," she didn't sound all that shocked actually.

I was still sitting lost in admiring my own assertiveness. "Why the court, are you suing me?" I said it just to humor her.

"No, cause when our child is born you'll have to pay child support."

I didn't go home with a smile that day. Or the next.

Overnight I went back to my old self. Even worse.

I freaked out and begged and pleaded with her to have an abortion. I tried everything to explain how nothing good could come of having it. I showed her my pay checks. I literally did everything I could for weeks, months to try and convince her to change her mind. Nothing worked, the suburb superman tail-spinned.

People noticed, but I didn't give a shit. I had other things to worry about.

Christina had turned into a completely different person. The girl that I took in the back room and to hotels late at night for rendezvous' was gone. Her flirtatiousness and sense of humor diminished. Our sessions faded, and my frustrations and problems came back.

I watched the weeks and months pass and Christina's stomach get bigger. The bigger it got, the more my head ached and the more I drank and went downhill. How can she be doing this to me? The sight of her every morning was tormenting me.

God, it was like having two Melanie's in my life. Both women were nagging me constantly. I couldn't go anywhere. At home Melanie got at me and at work Christina gave me stares and left me insulting little notes.

I held out as long as I could. But seven months into the pregnancy it was clear Christina wouldn't back down. I was tearing my hair out and banging my head in the bathroom. I couldn't sleep. I couldn't eat.

Wouldn't shower. It seemed like everything was coming down on me and I had nowhere to turn.

I'd sit up at night on the couch and sometimes wake Bobby up and take him out of his room. I'd set him on the floor in front of me and give him a few things to play with. Then I'd drink whatever I could get my hands on and just dream of being my boy. Being the innocent, naïve little creature that stumbled around and drooled on the floor in front of me without any worries whatsoever.

It got so bad one night, I was so drunk, I got down on all fours with my boy. And I actually tried to act like him. I grabbed at his blocks and fumbled around with them. I let drool run down my chin. I took my boy's head in my hands and pressed my forehead up to his and concentrated as hard as I could on switching bodies with him. I rolled on the floor and laughed until Melanie came in cause I was making too much noise. If I was sober I'd be embarrassed as hell.

If I was sober I wouldn't have done it to begin with.

But I was drunk and I did it and nobody was happy.

What have I become? Am I really this pathetic? Am I really wishing I was an autistic kid than a grown man with a family and a job? What's happened to me and my life?

I need to get a grip. I need to change.

I need to do, something.

-FOUR-

My heart is leaping and prancing like some gay rabbit in the woods. But every time I look back to see if she is following I see a trail of blood and veins. I've done everything I could to keep from getting caught but my fins are all shredded, like wheat. I can't have a kid, I've already got one of those popular dog pets. Maybe if people weren't so sophisticated we could have some fun and wag our tails too. My brain's hurting real bad and the cold, black lump in my chest is trying to beat but something's stopping it. The smiling images of her starting twisting and getting all distorted. The lips curled and curled until they were just endless rolls of lipstick. And the eyes. Those pupils grew darker and deeper and I turned my head to keep from looking down their endless spiraling staircases. I used all my strength to resist from leaning forward and kissing her skin.

"I can't go back, I can't!" Something in there is talking again. Me? Is that me? "I am talking?" "Am I talking." I hear me, I think.

It's one of those times when you wake up in your head before your eyes get a chance to open. I decided to keep them closed and try and shake the nonsense that was just going on in my head. Leftovers from some twisted dream.

I tried to think of nothing but my breathing: inhale, exhale, air goes in and air comes out. But for some unknown reason my neck is hurting real bad, like it's being stretched or something. I tried rolling it around on my shoulders and found it was like moving a fifty pound weight. Then I realized my chin was causing some sort of a sharp pain in my chest. What's going on here?

It took all my concentration to pull the eyelids up over my eyes. And when the thin fleshy curtains were drawn, I still couldn't see anything. Pitch black all around. Damn, I've woken up in the middle of the night with a cramped neck. My chin was still digging into my chest so I tried my best to slowly flex my neck and ease the pain.

Wait! Why's my chin digging into my chest in the first place? Something's not right. I thought I was maybe curled up in the fetal position for a second, but I couldn't feel my arms at my sides or my knees in my gut. I couldn't feel any of my body actually, besides the whole neck and chest thing. And when I tried to move my arms to roll over or something, I found myself restrained.

My sleepy head was coming together slowly and I was now aware enough to tell my arms were stretched out and restrained at the wrists. I should have been shocked back into full consciousness, but my mind was groggy and it was hard to concentrate. I felt for my legs. They hung together below me and something was tied around my ankles. I thought maybe I was panicking and imagining things cause I was still half asleep so I pulled on my arms remembering the cluttered room I fell asleep in and hoping I was maybe just trapped under some clothes or boxes. The harder I pulled the more something dug into the skin of my wrists and actually started hurting after a while. It was some thin, strong string or something.

I stopped tugging on my limbs and let the pain from the strings fade. My neck was working a little better now and when I pulled my chin out of my chest, I expected my head to roll back on the floor. Only there was no floor. Something was missing. Something that should have been a pillow or at least a hard surface, yeah a floor. Instead I swung my head back and forth, ignoring the stretching muscles supporting it, trying to find that floor thing, but instead feeling nothing but bare air.

I still couldn't see anything but black space and I was beginning to think maybe I was somehow too sleepy and out of it to comprehend the whole thing. I was just going to give up and go back to whatever it was I was dreaming about. But then my little groggy brain put two and two together and told me I must be floating in space. Like some kinda living, breathing, drooling satellite.

Work little mind, work. I pushed and pulled and tugged the thoughts through my head. Forcing myself to concentrate on my body and what was going on. But working with a brain that feels like it's been through one of those factory assembly machines with a hangover isn't easy. After focusing long enough, I sensed that somehow all my weight was in my legs and feet, it wasn't all dispersed evenly like when you lay on your back normally. And I never noticed before, but there were hard poles and things running along the back of my body. I struggled to pull the idea, like dragging a corpse, down the corridors of the nerves in my brain. I must, I must be laying straight up. Like vertical or something, definitely not normal on my back or side sleeping. How else could my head keep falling down and digging my chin into my chest?

But I wasn't on a floor. Why would I be sleeping straight up in the air, strapped to something? I tried to remember where I was before I fell asleep. Ok, some girls place, right. Yeah, that's right she brought you to her place and cleaned you up. And then she just left me in some cluttered living room, and that was it. So what, could something have happened after I fell asleep? No, no I'm just out of it, or maybe even having one of those dreams that feel just like real waking-world life.

I've had enough of this head filled, dizzying, space trip. I'm going back to sleep, or some other dream, or whatever. I let my head fall forward again and tried to ignore the pain from my chin.

I was doing my best to fall asleep and forget what I could only imagine was going on, when I heard something.

Now that the sound had already come and gone, I tried to figure it out. It came from over there, yes I think? Of course that didn't really matter right now cause every where I looked was just as dark. But there was definitely a sound. Something. Maybe an animal or an insect? I've questioned it so long I'm starting to ask myself if there was even a sound at all. Oh Jesus, just go to sleep.

When it's as pitch black as it is right now, it's hard to tell if your eyes are open or closed. When they're open, you can't see anything at all, so you keep trying to open them, which is impossible. It's just not natural to not be able to see anything like am now.

I closed my eyes and tried to shut it all out. But then I started questioning whether I had really shut my eyes. This is starting to drive me nuts. Then my body started feeling the effects of gravity. My arms were getting weaker from the stretching and my neck sorer. Even my legs weren't feeling so hot.

I started trying to shift around in whatever contraption I was tied into, but it was impossible, I was tied in good. My mind was almost operating normally now, but I was beginning to regret it. I was turning into a big withering, sweaty worm man tied to God knows what, in God knows where. I'm almost fully aware now, I started trying to squirm my way out. I tried curling my wrists and probing my fingers at the strings that bounded me tightly. I even bend my ankles and pointed my toes upward trying touch something.

I could feel someone in the space with me. I was almost fully awake now and was doing my best to keep up the progress. I wanted to talk and ask what was going on, but I couldn't find the words. I squinted and strained my eyes to try and find some light in the darkness. Find an outline of a person and prove to myself I wasn't nuts. Or maybe I wanted to be nuts, yeah, having some kind of a nutso dream. Then I could wake up in that cluttered little room, have a nice breakfast, get a new pair of clothes and be off on my merry way.

I could definitely feel a presence. I haven't seen or heard anything, but I felt it. Wait! There it is! Something moved. I swear! I saw something in the corner over there. Is it? Did something really move or is my mind playing tricks on me? I tightened my eye muscles as hard as I could trying to pick up the faintest ray of light bouncing off the space in front of me.

I thought if I strained any harder I'd bust a nerve and just then the dead silence was broken by sound of something clicking behind me.

Click, click. Rats? Long nails tapping? A push pen, what the hell is that sound? It almost sounded familiar, I must know that sound from somewhere. I wanted to yell at it, scream out a question or threat. But my vocal system would have no part of it.

Suddenly there was warmth growing in my fingertips and warming its way down my arms. The same thing was happening in my toes. Something was appearing in the darkness at the same time. A small, soft red light was appearing in front of me. It started as a small dot, but began growing into a circle. And the warmth continued to spread through my body, like I was being dipped into warm water real slow or something. The heat reached my torso and I felt good all over, like I was in a hot tub, yet wasn't a drop wet. I think? The heat start working its way up to my head and almost instantly my neck, arm and chest pain went away. Physically but not mentally comfortable. I stared curiously, at this new red circle. An opening?

Then I saw him. Her? It. A figure stepped into the red circle. It was like a spotlight in space, there must be a floor. I watched the figure point it's head back up at me and walk around the red circle as though it was deciding on what to do. Should I say something?

"Hey," I said in a normal voice.

The person looked up at me.

"Hey, what's going on? Who are you? Let me down." Ok so maybe I fired too many away at once. "Please?" the figure went back to its walking around in the red circle.

I don't really want to call it a figure but I have no other choice. I know it's human and all cause it has two legs and arms and a head, but that's about it. I can't even tell the sex. It's covered head to toe in a slick black rubber suit. Leather? Latex? The face was covered in the same black material.

I want to say I see breasts, so I could be sure it's a woman, but the problem is there is something strapped on the front of their chest. It's a like a box with stuff all over the front. Maybe buttons and knobs all over it or something.

"What's that on your chest?"

The figure stopped pacing again, faced me, then looked down at the box and twisted one of its knobs. A row of white lights along the side of the box lit up and blinked.

"Ok, I don't know what you want from me? I don't have anything. Why don't you just let me go? I don't even know you."

The figure walked out of the red circle and disappeared immediately. I couldn't see anything that wasn't right in front of me. The room was pitch black in every direction.

"Hey, come back! Don't leave me here!"

I shut up for a second and listened to the footsteps walk around somewhere off to the side of me. There was the sound of something being pulled until it sounded like it broke and then there was a scraping sound, like something being dragged on the floor.

And then it came back. The human, the figure this time it was pushing a large black box in front of it.

"What's that?"

The little human pulled out object after object and set them on the ground in front of me. Then there were bottles and a small box, finally the plastic human dragged out an armful of wires or cables from the box.

"What's all this stuff for?" I asked.

The figure didn't answer, no surprise, but kept sorting out the wires and when it was finished pushed the box out of sight again.

I stared at the figure hunched over its pile of stuff working hard at attaching some of the objects and weaving wires and cables together.

"What's all this stuff for?" Wait, didn't I just ask that?

I don't like being ignored, no one does, even if it is by something with no face or mouth. This has all the pieces for a perfect nightmare. Deep black unknown surroundings, claustrophobia, tied down to what I can only guess is a giant cross and this crazy looking mute plastic looking figure that keeps walking around this bloody light circle planning something. And what's all that electronic stuff for?

The black creature wouldn't answer me. It kept sorting and twisting and connecting wire after wire. Occasionally it would stop and play with a knob on its chest then go back to the wires.

After a whole strew of wires, and what I would call electric shit, was assembled and laid out in front of me resembling a thick chord of twisted cable, the silent creature turned its attention to me. It opened a new box and removed a container of something. That something inside was cold and sticky and the creature started spreading it all over my exposed abdomen.

I'm looking directly at it's faceless costume as it works on me. I don't see a seam or a zipper. Probably in the back. The shape of the body, more female than male. Could also be a teenager, I doubt it.

"Ok, what is going on now, huh?" I asked even though I knew I wouldn't get an answer. "Still not talking, eh?" I'm getting impatient.

"You're quieter than my wife in bed."

I thought I saw the creature wince but it was hard to tell.

"Trying to make conversation," I said. "seeing as I don't have anywhere I can really go. So not even one word then?"

The figure got to work attaching one end of the chord to my sticky abdomen. There were some sort of clamps on the end of the chord it used to pinch to my skin. I felt the pressure but it didn't hurt.

"What's that?"

I'm starting to lose my shit with this thing. It was probably that girl who 'rescued' me. I have to assume it's her. What was her name? Sam? She looked strikingly like Christina. I fell asleep in her place, under her watch. This could turn out to be worse than what I was going to get by those bastards in that alley. "What is that!" is she going to murder me? Torture me? I don't care, I don't want to be a part of it. This isn't a joke.

I pulled on my wrists, testing the strength of the string. I wriggled my fingers and tried to find a knot. I tried to form my hands into points to slide them free. Nothing worked, I was tied in good. Too good. My wrists were burning, probably cause they were bleeding from pulling on them too hard. The skin at my ankles was starting to pinch and hurt like hell. But I kept on fighting the restraints. I had rage on my side.

The bitch. The sick evil bitch. Why the hell would she do this to me? Revenge for all the sick shit those other men did to her? I'm not like them. "I'm not like those guys! Why are you doing this to me? Why?" I yelled at her.

The more I yelled, the harder I struggled. I kept it up for a minute or two, I think. My sense of time must be off. My sense of everything is off right now. I can't take being in the darkness like this. This isn't normal darkness. This is fucking weird ass outer space middle of nowhere darkness. I can't see the Goddamn walls and I'm strapped to this, this metal cross.

And that girl just keeps staring at me! I feel another burst of anger and energy coming on.

"Agghhhh! Do something or I'm going to go nuts!" I tried to break free by using all the muscles in my arms and chest. I felt the muscles fibers contract under my skin and felt the pressure pulling on my bones. I kept pushing it. I'm breaking out of this thing right now! I won't stop till I'm out!

I pulled on my arms harder and harder. "Arrrgghhhh!" All the muscles in my face were crunching up and sweat was running down my forehead and burning my eyes. I bit down on my tongue to fight the burn and tasted blood.

My head filled with blood and I thought it would burst but I kept pushing it. The blood filled my mouth and my head starting hurting. Keep pulling, keep pulling. I felt myself passing out and forced myself to use my last remaining strength for one last good pull.

I squeezed my arms and chest as hard as possible. I felt my ribs bend out and then it happened. The thing behind me started shifting. It was bending! It was moving, I was doing something! I'm getting out of this thing. "Ahhhhh ha!" I heard something in my shoulder make a snapping sound then my whole arm went numb.

Shit! What the hell happened? I looked at my arm in a state of panic and realized the girl was walking towards me. She had something in her hand. I had just enough time to make out a syringe before she stuck the needle into my side and pushed a bright white liquid out of the cylinder.

By the time she was sliding the needle back out, I felt my energy surge begin disappearing. My muscles went limp and my body started sagging forward. All that progress was lost. It became too hard to hold my head up, and my neck gave in and let my head fall forward smacking my chin back into my chest like how I woke up. I wanted to yell at her. Cuss her out and demand she tell me what she just injected in me, but I couldn't find the strength to open my mouth.

It was as if all my body just decided to give up. What the hell was in that syringe?

I could tell the girl was walking around in front of me and I did my best to roll my eyes up towards her. It was useless, every muscle in my body was limp. Jesus Christ.

How long has it been since I've had real control. How long has it been since I was able to move my legs and arms at my own free will. I know it must have been just hours, but it seems like longer. A lot longer. Maybe days or months. I've been in this state for too long. It's driving me insane. The human body wasn't meant to be operated like this.

Why are you doing this to me? What did I ever do to you? Nothing! What can you possibly get out of this? It makes no sense to me.

The girl was by my side and had her hands on my head and was shifting it around. Not only have I lost my physical strength, but I can feel myself losing mental strength too. It's like I've just become too lazy to feel anger with her. I'm becoming indifferent. What's going on? What was in that injection?

I could feel my panic and curiosity subsiding with the rage. I'm just in this accepting state of mind. Who cares what was in that syringe. What difference does it make?

Even thought I am completely aware of what's going on, this girl who obviously took advantage of me, I'm finding myself not caring. I don't care if I'm tied to this thing anymore. I don't care if I haven't seen daylight in God knows how long. I don't care if this girl's got me prisoner in some dark room. I don't care if she's pulling my head up and strapping it to the pole so I can see what's in front of me again. I don't care about that light on the floor in front of me. That hypnotic dark red circle of light.

It's strange, I think it might even be pulsing. I didn't think about it before, but when I was going nuts a few minutes ago, that spot was pulsing fast, and now it's definitely slowed down. Is it in sync with my heartbeat or something else? So slow, so smooth. It's so relaxing just watching it beat in the darkness. Like a big circle, light heart just beating away.

I heard the girl walking around and waited for her to walk on the red spot so I could see her. Go ahead, take as long as you want. I'm in no hurry.

I'm enjoying my relaxed state. I want it to last forever. This is better than any antidepressant, any buzz from alcohol any high from dope, any mind numbing television show or any post orgasm. This is complete and utter indifference. There is no happiness or sadness in my mind right now. No emotion whatsoever. No stress or panic, only the smooth flow of red liquid through the web of veins that line my brain. With every outward beat of the red spot, I feel a jet of blood travel up my neck, and into my brain where it rushes through the halls of blood vessels cleaning my mind of stressful thoughts and carrying them out of my mind and back down my neck. With every beat my mind becomes more cleansed of thoughts and I become more calm and relaxed. More calm, and more relaxed.

I could watch this red circle pulse for an eternity. This is perfect, being tied up here with nothing to worry about and just watching this red circle in the darkness. My own corner in space, I promise I won't bother anyone. I'll just stay here forever and my job will be to watch this spot. Watch it beat, outward and inward. So red and round. So smooth.

"Clank."

Did you hear that?

"Clank."

Oh look, I'm going up.

"Clank."

The metal thing I'm tied to is growing upward and that sound must be the gears or machine causing it. I'm going higher and higher and the dot is getting a little smaller and smaller below me.

I was so mesmerized with the spot I was completely unaware of what the girl had been doing the whole time. I didn't have a care about her or anything else besides that light and so she could have been doing anything in the darkness. All I knew now was that I was slowly being hoisted up into the darkness above me.

The metal cross kept growing higher and took me with it. It was hard to tell exactly but judging by the spot on the ground I'm guessing I'm maybe ten feet above it? When that girl gets back in the light I'll be able to tell for sure.

The cross raised a little more then stopped. I watched the red spot in silence for a little while longer before the girl returned to the red light.

I was too sedated and relaxed to even open my mouth and speak the words. I'm sure I could have, if I just wanted to. But it would take too much energy and effort. So I'll just be quiet and try to enjoy the red movement with her standing in the middle of it.

The chord attached to my stomach were dangling below me and I calmly watched as she grabbed at their ends and carried the loose ends with her in the darkness on the other side of the red spot. That beautiful red spot.

My muscles tightened and the euphoria disappeared. Something changed. I blinked quickly ending my dumbfound stare at the spot. Something happened inside me. I'm alert. A sensation. I felt plugged in. She plugged me in to something in the darkness.

I groaned. I had my vocal chords back.

"What did you plug me into? Goddammit! Tell me!" I yelled.

The red pulsing light quickened, my heartbeat I thought.

My stomach, where the twisted chord of cables is attached, that's where I felt it. Something was coming through it. Not matter, but an energy, a signal. I could feel it start heating up where it was attached to my stomach. Something quickly shot through my veins. I can't describe it. My finger tips and toes started tingling, even my ears and nose. Something. Something strange. Electric? I was focused on the sensation when every muscle in my body contracted instantly and the red dot disappeared.

I was opening my eyes. The red dot faded back into sight. Blink. What was that? A switch was thrown and everything went black again.

I opened my eyes. My nerves. I felt shocked. Electrified. My whole body jolted in place and the dot disappeared.

I opened my eyes to the faded red dot. Light headed and hot all over. "Stop!" I think I yelled it, but I'm not sure. It all went black again.

She shocked me again sending me back and forth between unconsciousness. Each time I regained consciousness I felt worse. I was completely disorientated and my body was starting to feel fried. Then she let me hang. I just hung there. Waiting for the next electrocution. She did it, she zapped me. But it didn't knock me out like the last times. Instead it went straight to my dick.

I recoiled and arched my back as far as I could. It wasn't the electricity, it was the pain that shot at me right between the legs. "Agghhhh!" I know I screamed that time. "Aghh!" she did it again. My body was twisting in pain. I tried to shake the electric chord from my abdomen between shocks. It was useless the thing was firmly attached.

She sent a hard sustained jolt that made my dick burn and eyes roll backward.

My penis felt blistered and worn. I was sure she couldn't do any more damage to it. But the chord thing started up again. What the hell!?

She tortured me for who knows how long. The yelps grew louder till finally I was screaming like an animal. I still couldn't make words out of my yells, just primal gorilla like screams.

Please stop, please, please. I've replaced my earlier threatening thoughts with begging. I'll do anything just stop hurting my penis. My whole waist and thighs burned and I'm sure my penis was fried before she finally stopped.

My yelling started dying down to little yelps. I tried to look down to see if my penis was still there but I couldn't see below my blurry cheeks.

I wanted to close my eyes and pray this was the end, that she would somehow just let me go. She'd lower me to the ground, untie me and shove me out some door and I'd be free.

I can't believe a girl did all this to me.

Where'd she get that? The girl was standing over a new box and opening it. I must lost track of her for a second. Maybe I did close my eyes and pray just now? I watched her open the box revealing a row of syringes. Each one was filled with a light colored liquid.

She removed one of the syringes and stuck the needle right into the chord. She pushed all that glowing needle juice out of the chamber and into the cable, then stepped away.

Oh shit!

I stared into her faceless head. My eyes grew wide and begged and pleaded for her to stop. Don't do anything, please!

She punched a button and sent the green stuff shooting up the cable towards my body. I didn't see it, but I felt it hit that tender piece of tissue hanging between my legs.

Almost immediately my penis and testicles felt like they silently exploded. I let out a yell so loud it seemed to echo in the space around me. I couldn't be sure without looking, but I imagined my dick must be gone, leaving a few strands of veins and mangled tissue dangling between my legs with two deflated sacks of smoking pubes.

I was in a state of absolute shock. So stunned I couldn't blink or think. I started getting light headed and thought I was going to pass out. My stomach turned a few times and I found myself wishing I would faint, of course dying wouldn't be so bad right about now either. But I didn't. I survived and remained conscious enough to watch the girl push the box out of sight.

I'm in too much shock to yell at her to let me down or even moan. I don't know what to think or do right now. I just need to breath. My heart was pounding fast and sweat was seeping out of every one of my pores at once, causing tingling sensations all over my body. The red dot was pulsing like crazy.

So this is what it's like when you go into shock, I wondered? I wonder how long I'll have before I get electrocuted to death. My crotch and thighs were completely numb. I couldn't feel pain, heat or even blood spewing out of some gapping hole where my dick used to be. So I just hung there in the darkness not really thinking anything at all. Just kind of hanging there staring blankly at the red pulsing dot which seemed to be slowing down with my heart beat.

The girl returned, but I didn't even flinch. My eyes saw her walk in the center of the circle again but my brain didn't really give a shit.

She looks like she's smaller? I mean shorter? At first I saw the changes but I didn't really care. The slick black suit had been replaced with a long flowing black dress and the seamless head mask was gone but there was something else covering her head, like a cloth. She stood in the center of the light and I could see it wasn't just a cloth hanging over her head, it was a veil. Then it came together, she was in a black wedding dress or a funeral dress. While I was staring at her completely confused and thinking she must seriously be nuts and probably acting out some fantasy, then without warning she threw back her veil and revealed her face.

Melanie! It was the face of Melanie. A sickly sad looking Melanie complete with wedding makeup gone bad. Her eyes were all smudged with black eye shadow and even the dark lipstick looked like it was poorly applied? But that was nothing compared to the look on her face and in her eyes. The pale face and deep eyes said it all. She had the look of a woman who was in sever pain and at the same time was filled with rage. Enough rage to kill.

I can't be sure, but it looks like she might be snarling because her nostrils are getting pinched back and the corners of her lips are curling down.

Melanie, Melanie thank God it's you! "Melanie!" I managed to squeak out. "What are you doing? Get me down, thank God you're here." My voice was weak and my words barely understandable. Of course there is no possible way this woman could be Melanie but I have to accept that my mind has gone through enough shock and trauma that its beginning to hallucinate. But she looks so much like Melanie.

I tried to squint and get as detailed a look as I could but the woman pulled the veil back over her face and stepped backwards to the center of the red dot. Melanie?

I felt the chord in my stomach heat up. Oh God not this again.

I thought she would immediately start sending bolts of some sort of pain up the cable and into my chest, but instead she started some kind of dance to unheard music. And honestly it was just as hypnotizing as the smoothly red pulse she was dancing on. Her movements were slow and methodical with her arms stretched out and waving gently as if in a breeze.

This must be a different girl. At first I thought maybe that rescuing girl had put on some sort of mask and managed to pull of looking like Melanie, but that would be impossible. Now I'm almost positive this is Melanie. Besides Melanie always was a good dancer. The looks and the movements, this must be Melanie.

So they're in on it together. The girl and Melanie. I was putting the whole thing together in my mind, like assembling a puzzle and forming a clear picture from what was once just a bunch of scattered thoughts. That girl who saved me, the one who dragged me away from the club she must have been Christina. With a makeover or something. And Melanie had gotten her to drug me into a deep sleep. Then Christina and Melanie took over and tied me up to this cross, this insane torture device. And I have no fucking clue where I am. I could be anywhere from some garage in the middle of the suburbs to an abandoned office downtown.

They were crucifying me.

But where did they get all this electronic stuff? Christina, of course! I never saw her place, never really knew that much about her. This could be hers. This is probably even her place. That would explain it. Or at least comfort me enough into getting over all this paranoia about being held up in space by a sadistic freak.

There was still one thing I couldn't figure out. How did they know I faked my death. I didn't tell a soul. No one could have known I pulled it off so well I thought.

Maybe there's hope I can get out of this then. Sure, Christina's got a kid and probably neighbors. They must have heard me yelling earlier. The cops are probably on there way right now. Just hang in there a few more minutes and there will be sirens followed by the swat team breaking down doors and letting the light shine all over your tortured naked body.

103

Unless Christina lives in a place where's there's no neighbors. That could be true too. I mean we lived miles outside the city. There were plenty of woods and a mountain range that separated our small city from the big metropolis. Christina could have one of those places out in the woods, like a hermit. But didn't she say she needed money for rent was it? That would mean she's in an apartment or a rental house.

I was busy trying to sort things out in my head and hadn't noticed Melanie's dance had died and now the bride of death was looking up at me hanging ten feet above her and stretched her left arm up towards me and pointed at me with her ring finger. I could clearly see the wedding ring I slipped on her finger years ago in front of our family and friends all wishing us, no not even wishing, knowing we'd have a happy life together. Because we went so well together. Because we were so in love, we would have died for each other. And I watched Melanie hold that finger up towards me and with her other hand she pulled that veil back off her face revealing that pale face made up with all the black makeup, only now the black eyeliner was running down her cheeks and made it look like she had been crying black tears.

Then as I hung here, strapped to this machine, my once lovely wife who I had vowed to spend the rest my life cherishing while slipping that ring over her finger, feeling dizzy on the altar with love and attention in front of a church full of wedding guests, took that same finger and ring that was pointed at me now and brought it down into her open mouth. And without even blinking she brought her white teeth down hard, hard enough for me to hear the sicking crunch of her finger bone being ground between her teeth. And as I winced in pain for her, she gave me a smile of teeth quickly turning dark red and jerked her head to the side giving the final tear needed to pop her finger off her hand.

I can't believe what I just saw. With my own two eyes that feel like they're ready to fall out from gravity and shock. My stomach sank and I felt my throat muscles tightened, then warm burning fluid came rushing up and I threw my head forward as I vomited all over the red lighted floor in front of Melanie and the rest dribbled on my bare chest.

"Melanie, what, why," I couldn't find the words to say anything more.

She just stood there grinning at me then she spit the finger, with the ring still on it, out into the darkness. And with blood running down her chin and her eyes full of fire she disappeared back into the dark.

I knew what was coming, pain, only I thought it would be sent in the form of a fireball shooting up the cable and pounding into my gut. Instead what I got was something deeper, something unexpected.

It didn't come in the form of a fireball. It wasn't even the zig zag of electricity driving up the cable. At first I wasn't sure, but I felt I felt something in my fingers and toes. Then I was positive. It did start there and it was spreading. It's a tightening feeling, like my muscles are contracting. It felt as if every muscle in my body was tied to my heart and my heart was pulling everything in. All the muscles in my body got tighter and it really began to hurt. I was collapsing in on myself. I looked at my arms and expected to see them crunching up towards my body like balloons deflating. But they were still there, stretched out like I was flying. Oh God, its tightening. Everything, every muscle even the bones, all of me is being reeled into my chest. And now it's hit my neck and brain, oh God my brain. My neck has turned into some kind of drain and my brain is starting to spin, spinning in my skull as its getting washed down the drain of my neck. A headache quickly formed and my eyeballs rolled

105

back uncontrollably then my tongue felt like it was sliding back down my throat. What the fuck is going on!?

My thoughts, my thoughts aren't coming ot right. It's getting hrd to fcus n, on what I'm thinking. The words, the sounds ar getig all scambled. I'm trying to stay focused. Concentrate. All I can think of is all my nerves and cells trying to fight to stay in place and fighting to resist whatever was pulling them slowly towards the center of my new center of gravity, my heart.

My heart, my heart has turned against me. I pictured a cold black lump of fatty tissue pumping blood as dark and thick as oil through my arteries. The heart has malfunctioned and instead of pumping rich red blood full of oxygen to my demanding cells, it's sucking me in. All of me. It's pumping and pumping and devouring my blood and flesh like a monster festering inside my chest behind my ribcage.

I'm panicking and breathing faster, I can't see clearly cause my eyes are rolled back but I think that red spot is pulsing faster and I feel my heart beating harder. I'm straining my eyes to the side to make sure I still have my arms. My Goddamn body's collapsing in on itself!

Holy shit, holy shit. The pressure is becoming unbearable. I'm gasping at the air to scream but my lungs have stopped working, I don't know how I'm getting oxygen but its not from my lungs, they've deflated and crumpled up into slimy, veiny prunes in my chest. All the muscles in my arms and legs are separating from the bones and sliding their way along my bones like slugs towards my sickening traitor heart.

Even the penis which I was sure had blown to pieces feels like its been sucked back into my torso, worse than any ice cold water could do. Oh God its tormenting! The pain! Stop! Stop it Melanie you're killing me!

My brain is spinning faster, I can't take it, my muscles, my bones, my joints grinding against each other, bones straining to keep from crumbling, the pressure, pulling everything, all of me, the center, the heart, my heart, burning, not pumping, sucking, sucking me up, eating me up, I'm dying, Melanie, stop, please, I'm begging you, I'm sorry, please, my heart, words, can't think, only pain, this isn't right, I'm sorry.

And then like that, as if someone just flipped a switch, and Melanie probably did just that, the pain, the suffering, the collapsing feeling, it all just went away.

I was so shocked I could barely let out a few gasps of relief and begin my mental recovery of what just happened when the collapsing happened again. Instantly my heart began sucking me up like a black hole again. And then it stopped. She was playing with me. Melanie was controlling my pain from the other end of that cable. She did it again and I tried to yell but my tongue was rolling down my throat and my teeth felt like they were sinking in my gums like quicksand.

Then it stopped.

"Melanie! Stop, please!" I yelled as fast as I could before she could do it again.

She did it.

I mouthed at the air like a fish out of water.

When it was over I begged again. "Melanie please," tears from pain and apology were forming in the corners of my eyes. "Please Melanie. I'm sorry don't do this. I don't know how much more I can take."

But she sent me into a world of pain again. And I came out again. This went on, I don't know how many times. With me begging and pleading harder every time I came out. Because every time I went it seemed like the pains and pressure grew worse.

I couldn't have deserved this for cheating. This is just nuts. Borderline murder.

Melanie had me at the point where I was yelling apologies and begging with tears. I seriously didn't think she would let me live. I thought it would end with her flipping that switch and just walking away.

But she didn't leave me in constant torture. The chord stopped and didn't start back up again. I breathed in relief. Big gulps of air and I looked over at my arms to make sure I was all in one piece.

I felt abandoned up here. I am ok with that right now. I never would have expected them capable of this. Even of thinking of the sick and twisted things they pulled on me. Christina, well maybe her. She was nuts to begin with I guess. But Jesus Christ Melanie! You, you're so, so innocent and definitely not violent. This isn't like you at all. What happened? I felt the answer but didn't even want to think it. I happened. It was me. Could what I have done to her possibly pushed her this far?

No. Not in a million years. People cheat on their spouses all the time and they don't go nuts and torture the adulteress to the brink of death. They kill them, yes. But torture no. Something's happened to Melanie and it wasn't just my affair with Christina. Maybe Christina had an influence over her. That's the only other thing I can think of.

Ow! What was that? I felt a sharp tingling pain around my stomach then it quickly went away.

I looked down to see the thick chord of twisted wires and tubes connected to my body come to life. The cable lit up and created an eerie red glowing line that started at my belly button and disappeared as it traveled off into the darkness in front of me. I still have no idea what the other end is attached to.

Then came noises.

I can hear low hums and what sounds like the shifting of gears in the distance.

I witnessed in awe and horror as a rumble louder than any thunder rattled my ears and everything around me. The sounds didn't die off. It was so loud enough to cause the cross I was on to shake. This Goddamn room I'm in is coming to life. As dazed and confused as I was earlier I seemed to be logical enough to realize I wasn't really truly in outer space. I'm probably just in some huge pitched black room like a warehouse. And this is probably just some large machinery inside being turned on.

I listened closer hoping I could figure out what kind of a warehouse or factory I was in by dissecting the types of I could hear.

Far off in the darkness was a constant and low rumble. There was a dry scraping sound like an old engine trying to turn. There was a louder sound like the sound of a train in the distance or a large air conditioner blowing on high.

I am reminded of the machinery smells that first hit me when I awoke.

I felt a blast of cold air and goose bumps explode all over my body, as I felt my muscles immediately start twitching.

"Clank. Clank."

The sound of a large gear advancing slowly.

"Clink. Clink."

Followed by a smaller one.

I want to yell out for help but with all this noise no one would hear me, and even if someone did it would probably just be Christina or Melanie. Jesus Christ its loud, this has to be like a manufacturing plant or something.

The darkness around me grew louder as more machines turned on and joined the industrial orchestra of grinding metal. It sounds like every form of transportation having a collision at once. It's that bad.

And I'm stuck in the middle of all this noisy darkness with this red circle of light that's now going nuts and pulsing rapidly.

And then I screamed. Louder than I ever screamed in my life. Not because the noise was a few decibels away from bursting my eardrums, or because I'd finally lost it after being tortured by my wife and mistress. No, I screamed because something out there in the darkness caused a flash of light, as bright and quick as lighting, and for a millisecond my surroundings were lit up like a stage, and that millisecond was all I needed to see I wasn't in any warehouse or factory I could ever imagine.

Forget the idea that there are machines lined up on some smooth factory floor with empty conveyor belts going into big silver boxes and coming out with junk at the other end. Throw that classic cartoon factory idea out the shit hole. I wish I never caught that glimpse. This is no factory. This is a nightmare.

If I hadn't seen it with my eyes I wouldn't have believed it. Giant, and I mean gigantic gears, pistons, pulleys, poles and odd metallic shapes the size of houses for as far as the eye can see, in every direction. Above, in front of me and on all sides the moving metal goes on until it becomes just a big blur of rusted gray. Even below me, where I assumed a floor, is more of what's above. The only flat surface is the red circle. In every direction the machinery operates like clockwork.

I feel like a bacterium trapped behind the face of a clock.

The flashes of light continued at an erratic rate like a strobe light gone schizo. My vision was flooded with the absurd machine images. I have no idea where I am. I am utterly lost, both in space and in thought. The sounds thundered and the lights flashed and in my mind I wondered where the fuck I was.

The red spot below me had stopped pulsing and was now stable. No wait, it's still moving. It's moving outward. I mean its getting bigger. The red dot is growing. It's taking up more and more space in front of me. Wait a second! It's not growing, I'm getting closer! The thing I'm strapped to is lowering me down face first onto the red spot.

And all I can wonder is how did I, the classic father in the suburbs, end up in this twisted nightmare, crucified in a giant machine being lowered towards this red light.

The red dot which I now see as the cervix grew. And my metallic cross lowered me closer until my body was hovering a few feet above what was once a red circle stage where my torturers stood.

The edges of the cross quivered madly and in the very center of the bright red blood spot, a little black dot appeared. It appeared and began to widen. That's definitely a cervix and this is giant machine is a mechanical womb.

The cervix is opening!

It started off the size of a pinhole on the below my chest. And at first it was too dark for me to see anything other than just a black spot growing slowly. But after it was big enough for me to put my fist through I could see something was on the other side.

I couldn't tell what at first, but the more that hole stretched the more

I was able to down into it. I want to say I'm looking at something with a lot of little lights. Little dot lights. Maybe stars? Is that a little window into space I'm looking through. Maybe it's a black hole, no those are pure black. This, this has lights.

The hole continues stretching and it has me so interested my ears have completely shutdown and I don't hear the thundering machines at work around me.

If I wasn't strapped to this cross, I could kneel down on that red cervix and put my head right through the hole and see the other side. Patience, it's still growing you'll see it soon enough.

I'm utterly terrified and sicken with amazement at the same time. I am completely overwhelmed with curiosity and adrenaline. Everything my body has gone through in the past hours, minutes, who knows, is completely forgotten. All the pain and suffering, all that is behind me. I am moving forward now, into the future. I am witnessing the most amazing rebirth ever. My own.

Saliva builds up in my mouth and I'm concentrating so hard on peering through the hole that the liquid slips through the crack of my lips and I begin drooling on the cervix below.

Grow hole! Grow faster! I want, I need to see what's on the other side. I subconsciously tug on my wrists even though they're strapped in place I want to reach out and touch it.

"Ah ha! It's widening!" I even let out a yell so my machine audience can hear. "Ha! It's opening, for me!"

It's black on the other side. Space with no stars. My own personal porthole to outer space.

The cervix continued to stretch until it was more than wide enough to fit me. Once it stopped, my placenta cross began vibrating again. The motion built up until it was shaking wildly and I shook with it. My electronic umbilical chord turned black and detached. I watched as my end fell halfway through the cervix and dangled there in space. I will be there soon.

The cross jolted me towards the opening and back up again. I felt the straps around my wrists and ankles loosening. This thing was shaking me so hard I was coming free. I felt a sense of panic flow over me. Instantly the sounds of the machinery working came back into my ears. The sound was louder than ever. Suddenly I didn't want to be set free. I didn't want to fall through the cervix. All the curiosity was gone. All that was left was fear. I'm deathly afraid of what's on the other side of this hole.

Don't break straps please! Please! God please! Don't let me fall through this thing. I was almost on the verge of praying for Christina and Melanie to come back.

One of my wrists slipped through the loosened strap.

"Ah!" it caught me by surprise. The cross didn't stop its jerking. I tried to reach behind me to find something to hold on the cross. I'll find a way to keep from falling. I franticly groped behind me, praying for a bar or joint, something stable I could wrap my fingers around. I found nothing and one of my legs broke free.

Now with hand searching I had a leg kicking wildly. There was nothing to grab behind me. There was a smooth pole running along my back, but it was too wide around for me to get a grip.

Maybe I can get both arms around it. Ok how am I going to do this? I didn't have a chance to figure it out because my other arm was shook free.

"Aghh! Shit, shit, please God! Please God!"

My whole body fell forward. I'm now left dangling halfway through the cervix with one ankle still tied to the cross. My body is swinging back and forth and jolting up and down.

I don't know why, but I tilted my head back so I could look straight out into the darkness, an eternity of space. Is that what I am going to fall into? Is that what I am being born into?

"No!" I wont let it happen God. If you wont do anything, I will. It's in my control now. I used all my strength to tighten my abs and pull myself up. I grabbed my leg that was still tied in and used it to hold me up. I swung my free arm up towards the wide pole that formed the center of the cross. It was way out of reach but I was desperate and continued to reach for it. "Please!"

My hand caught hold of something. The straps that held my other leg! I tightened my fingers around it. I'm not letting go for anything. I was just in time, my last leg that was strapped in popped loose and left me hanging by my fingers.

I quickly grabbed the straps for the second leg so I was now holding on with both arms. "Ha ha! You're not getting rid of me!"

There was a quick jerk downward and like hand wringing off water, the metal cross flung my body into the darkness.

I fell toward the endless void of space, the air sucking my screams up all the way.

-FIVE-

I continued to fall through the darkness naked and screaming. Eventually the wind sucked all the air out of my lungs and I could scream no more.

The falling lasted forever. Or at least it seemed like forever. There was nothing around me really to focus on. Absolutely nothing. I was able to turn my body halfway over as I fell to look above me. I expected to see some kind of a structure where I fell out of. But no, it was pitch black like outer space with no stars. I rolled back over so I was falling face first, the cold wind pounded my face and stretched the skin. I tried to look below me, to see where I was falling, but it was too hard to open my eyes with all the wind blowing straight into them. I somehow managed to squint but all I saw was darkness again.

Again.

And so I fell like this. Forever. Or at least it seemed like forever.

There was nothing really for me to think of. Absolutely nothing. I was able to turn a few thoughts over in my mind to reflect on where I'd been recently. I expected to see nightmarish memories and terror in my mind. But no, it was pitch black like outer space with no stars. I rolled my thoughts around in my head to forget about the past and focus on the future, what was in front of me, but instantly my mind was swarming with visions. I somehow managed to fixate on one vision in particular, but as soon as I caught it, it was gone and my mind was filled with darkness again.

No sense of time passing. Total darkness. Complete disorientation. Am I falling inside my head?

After forever happened again and again, and after the cold wind had blown against my flesh long enough to numb it and after I had been surrounded with darkness both inside and out for too long, I saw a light. It started off small, like a dot in the distance. It was hard to see at first because I had to squint, but the longer I focused on it, the more I could see it wasn't alone.

There were two, then three, no four. Half a dozen little lights way out in front of where I was falling. Before long there were too many to count and a large group of these little white lights were clustered in front of me. Like a ball of stars, and I was falling straight into the them.

I watched intensely as the cluster grew thicker and some lights even started to appear as a line. I was so engrossed in this sight that I completely ignored the sting of holding my eyes open wide in the wind and just stared in awe.

What is it? Is it an it? A creature? A cosmic phenomenon? And more importantly why am I falling towards it? Is it pulling me with gravity? I could only watch.

As time passed the cluster grew larger, which made sense if I was falling toward it. It was still hard to tell how far away I actually was because I have no idea what it is. It started out as a tiny light no bigger than a speck of sand. And it was now the size of my hand.

But the amazing thing was, was that it seemed to be growing at an increasing speed. A second ago I could barely fit my hand over it, now it was nearing twice the size of my hand. The lights were much denser and the lines were forming a perfect grid.

I could also see that I wasn't falling straight for the center of this thing, as I thought before. I could now tell I was falling more to the bottom of it, or at least to the edge of it.

Oh my God! That can't be what I think it is? Oh my God? Give it one more second then I'll know for sure. No wait, another second. Is it possible?

I am going to die for sure.

My mind is saying its not possible, but my wind burned eyes are showing differently. What I thought was maybe a cluster of stars is actually, God I can't believe it, a city. A metropolitan city. An electric lit-up downtown. A gigantic one that filled the sky in front of me more and more with each passing second.

But at the same time there is this huge patch of darkness surrounding the city where it looks like the downtown just ends, and that's where I was aimed. If the city were an island I'd be falling right where the shore is. Right for where the darkness and the downtown meet. The city now took up half my sight and the darkness the other half.

How could I be falling? How is this possible? Where did I fall from?

Of course I thought of these questions before, but now more than ever. At the rate I'm falling I won't have more than a minute left of thoughts anyway. So why waste them on pointless questions.

The end is speeding toward me, don't waste these seconds. Think thoughts that matter. Think of something that matters. I tried, but my brain just didn't want to work. I didn't get my lifetime flashing before my eyes like everyone always says. My mind just wanted to witness, to accept what my eyes saw like a t.v.

So I fell toward the city and my eyes picked up more and more detail. Skyscrapers reaching toward me, dark city park blocks, streetlight dots, flashing signs, car lights moving like ants even people.

And the next moment my body fell a million thoughts a second straight down into the darkness bordering the city.

And it all ended with limbs flailing and wet stuff splattering in every direction. Hard. My body slammed into the surface so hard I felt myself go right past the ground and sink like a drill bit straight down into the surface. And as fast as I hit, I began to slow down till I was motionless and floating. Yes, I'm floating. Floating up? How?

I bobbed out of what I thought was the ground only to find myself coughing up saltwater and kicking and swinging my arms side to side to keep my head up.

Holy shit, it's water! It's an ocean! I fell in the ocean! Water!?

My head bobbed up and down with the rolling waves. It took a minute for me to finish coughing up the water and another minute me to reorient myself with the city.

The lights. The lights, are right in front of me and the waves are pushing me in that direction. I can make out the outlines of buildings and even see some windows. I'd say maybe I'm a mile off shore at most?

Well I'll make it shorter with every stroke. So I began swimming towards the city lights, using the waves to help me push.

The water was freezing. My naked body shivered so hard I could barely move my arms. Muscles contracted spastically. I felt my nuts suck up into my waist for warmth. Heart slowed. The salt burned my eyes when water splashed my face. After a while my hands started burning then went numb. I was trying my hardest to paddle but it was worthless. I could barely keep my head afloat. I was pretty much a drowning rat. I think the only reason my shivering, naked sack of a body made it to shore an hour later was cause of the waves.

With the waves running over my body and my face half buried in sand and the starless space above, I just wanted to lay there forever listening to the sounds of the city and surf a few meters away.

The traffic, car horns, muffled voices, a stray dog even the sounds of police sirens are soothing right now.

The only reason I got up was because I was so cold, I was afraid my dick would freeze off and bones would crack.

So I crawled up the polluted beach littered with human waste and debris. I guess expecting a boardwalk was too much, the sand went right up to a grungy sidewalk that turned into an alley that opened up into a major downtown street. And guessing by the activity I'd say it was a lively eight pm on a Saturday night.

I was still ass naked and didn't want to draw any attention so I stayed in the alley and rummaged around in the garbage until I was able to put together an outfit of greasy damp clothes that didn't match.

Hey, I can't complain. You get tortured to the brink of death then ejaculated out into the sky where you miraculously survive a billion foot free fall. Fuck! I'm just lucky to have a couple legs to put these contaminated clothes on.

I stepped out of the alley and into the hustle bustle of a weekend night downtown full of life and excitement, or so I thought. Cars, people, lights and motion everywhere. At first I was too into myself to notice anything around me. Scattered thoughts of where I'd been, how I managed to survive, where would I go, and other bullshit floated through my mind while I put one foot in front of the other and made my way down the first block. People brushed past me and I rolled with their shoves, nothings changed since I left. Does it ever?

There's a lot I've gone through recently. And I'm not just talking the past few hours, even though that was bad enough. The past few weeks, months. you could even go so far as to say years. Just too much to digest. My problems or life I left behind.

The apartment, job, eighty-three thousand, gross, sixty-eight net, credit cards, student loans, in the red, my wife, beautiful, at one time, nagging, cold, frigid in bed, apathetic, lazy, mistress, good fuck, manipulative, conniving, pregnant, very pregnant, eight months, a bribe, I can't afford it, even deeper in the red, red, my children, offspring, a male and female, I don't even understand them, the girl, she hates me, my boy, my, mine, autistic, I'm jealous, my genes, he's innocent, pure, his own reality, jealous, then my unborn fetus, sitting in my mistress's uterus, breathing fluid, amphibian like, even more innocent.

I don't want any of it going through my mind right now. That's why I'm here. I left it all behind for a reason. Maybe a little later I'll sit down and make some sense of it. Right now I just want a break. Some time to myself. It's my mind and I want to think about thoughts I want. They can't control me all the time. I need a mental break. I don't want to think about anything. I should be dead. In pieces. I walk and think thoughts of nothingness. A blank mind. Traumatized from the fall and life. For some reason I didn't think too much on how I'd gotten here anymore. The fall. The machine, the girl. All of it were vanished from from my mind. I just didn't care. Sure I thought it was odd, but hell I figured probably just a bad dream still. One of those endless dreams that go on way too long. One hell of a lucid dream.

I keep my eyes squinted and use my sight just enough to avoid obstacles. But I don't look at anything, or anyone. I blur my vision. So as I walk I just stare at the backs of blur shapes. Foggy sports coats, pant legs, skirts, flyers and scraps of paper, empty cups, patches of black dirt, curbs, asphalt, cross walks, sewer caps, uneven concrete slabs, grease and piss stains, windows displaying cheap clothes, broken glass, homeless bags, sticky, hard. This city is just one giant Goddamn above ground sewer pipe getting trampled. Nothing's worth looking at. My bones felt cold so I rubbed my arms with fierce strokes and focused on warming myself.

I don't know how much time has passed since I last felt normal. I feel like I found where I belong, yet utterly lost in this strange city at the same time. Has something changed inside me? Why do I feel like this is somebody else's body? Someone else's mind? Am I just renting these thoughts at this moment? Questions, thoughts, philosophies about existence kept floating through my mind as I walked. One foot in front of the other. One thought and question followed another.

My thoughts weren't getting me anywhere. And neither were my steps. I looked around and saw I was standing at the foot of an intersection. The same as the intersection before it. Typical. Any downtown metropolitan city anywhere. Normally I just stare at the ground and follow the herd across the road when the time is right. But I looked up this time. Looked to see when the little red hand would turn into a walking man. And the first thing to catch my attention was a car that drove by. No, not just a car. A taxi.

Yeah, I know taxies are common. Not like this one though. Traffic is always congested on the city streets. So the taxi drove by slow enough for me to take a double, even a triple look. Then I just stared.

As the taxi rolled by, first thing that caught my attention was the cab was more black than yellow and white. Odd paint job. But I knew it was a taxi cause of the checkered paint and lit up little taxi sign on the roof. But a black cab I had never seen. Maybe it's a private one? As my mind digested the sight, I realized it was shaped a lot like a hearse. I stared. I was also able to see with perfect detail through the windshield, that the cabbie was wearing a gas mask. It doesn't end there. There was a tube coming out of the mouth of the gas mask and hanging right out the window. It would be one thing if the end was dangling loose out the window, but no. The tube continued all the way to the back of the hearse-cab, where the loose end was attached to the car's exhaust pipe. The car's exhaust pipe!

It's one of those things you look at, and even though you're staring straight at it, you just don't believe it.

I know I've got enough shit of my own to worry about, but Jesus fucking Christ! What the fuck is this guy thinking? I watched the back of the cab as it drove away. I couldn't take my eyes off the end of the pipe where the gas mask tube was attached. He'll be dead within a couple minutes of carbon monoxide poisoning. It's got to be a prank.

I probably would have kept staring if it wasn't for the person behind me who shoved me into the street to start crossing. I walked the crosswalk with the rest of the street herd. I thought about how that driver was breathing his fumes while driving one more time, then went back to my mindless bullshit. Whatever, it's his lungs. His life.

And this is my life. I need to move on. Get over the facts. I'm lucky. Lucky I've got a second chance. I can put everything behind me and move on. A lot of people can't do that. I can say 'fuck you' to my wife, mistress and job. I'm gonna start fresh. I need to find a hospital or something. Just get myself checked out. Make sure there's no internal bleeding or anything. Next thing I need is to start coughing up blood and pissing colored shit.

Then someone threw up on me. It came from the side. There was a gut wrenching sound, like a big burly man burping and food being thrown down a hatch and then there it was, bits of half chewed food covered in saliva all running down my greasy polyester dumpster pants.

I didn't even flinch.

Why should I?

I didn't even have to stop really, or look up to see what ugly faced bloke this shit came out of.

But I did.

And I shouldn't have.

He was a big guy. Huge. In all directions. Face looked like meaty balloon. And he's the owner of one of those shitty little hotdog stands you see propped up on every street corner, or next to every overflowing trashcan or late night dance club. We made eye contact for about a second. I looked into dark tiny eyes buried in a fat face full of hair, grime and vomit. Eyes that somehow appeared strangely helpless. He probably looked back into a face of indifference and exhaustion. Then he looked away, and I watched as he pushed an entire hotdog into his gaping mouth. His lips struggled to close and suck in the last millimeters of the pink wiener. I'm not sure if I saw him chewing, but his swollen cheeks sunk in as I saw his neck swallow the mouthful of butcher scraps and cheap white bread. Then he faced me again, gave a sickening cross-eyed stare, rolled his eyes back and opened his mouth.

I moved out of the way just in time to see pink and white chunks blow all over the side of some woman who stepped right in my place. She didn't even break her pace and just kept walking as if the regurgitated, reused, rejected meat chunks running down her skirt were invisible.

The hotdog vendor stuffed another dog in his chops.

God this city is getting weirder every day.

That or I'm just not catching on.

Nope, has to be weirder.

I quickly jumped back in rhythm with the walking crowd. Didn't want to stand near that vendor long enough to pick up an unheard of case of air-born food poisoning. Jesus Christ! What the fuck was going on with that hotdog vendor? And what about that woman who got puked on? Who was more twisted? The puker, or the pukee? Why don't any of these people care? I kept up with the pace of the crowd.

I don't need this bullshit right now. For fuck's sake people. I survived a free fall. I need to find a medic, a hospital. My organs are probably juiced. Just give me a break.

It hit me like an explosion.

For the first time I started paying attention to what was going on around me and not just the thoughts and visions in my head. The puking was one thing, but I never realized the whole time I've been walking around a city full of freaks. Every single person is involved in some sort of twisted scenario or action. Nobody broke a step or flinched except me.

I looked up.

Oh fuck.

All at once I realized what the city around me was made up of. It's dark, real dark, drab. There's barely any color anywhere. A desaturated city. Full of grays and black shadows, caught in a grayscale state. Right out of a film noire.

Light gray sidewalks lining dark streets, deep black rivers like tar. Rows of trees running down the street, look like they're made of concrete, extensions of the sidewalk with ashy white trunks and black leaves. Branching out a hundred times into deformed skeleton-like hands reaching up. Gritty and rough. Glossy buildings, towering dark structures. Thousands of feet of twisted wires and cables snaking through steel I-beams. Black tinted windows hide what's going on inside. Dark ivy grows like poisoned veins up the sides of the buildings. A dark mist crawls out from even darker alleys and sewer caps like ghostly figures floating up from the pavement. White dots, that can only be small animal eyes, glow from dark corners behind dumpsters and boxes.

Now that I'm picking up details I'm noticing all the city lights are glowing a white light. Street lights, street level windows, headlights, all glowing white. Cars are all black, like rows of hearses. A continuous funeral procession in every direction. Big beetles can be seen scurrying around the gutters leaving a slick black trail of insect fluid behind them. Cracks in the building bleed a thick dark liquid. It runs down the sides of the buildings, following the cracks and making it's way like running mascara and tears to the gutter. In the gutter runs a thick stream of the stuff giving off a putrid steam.

The sky above. All of this, this ghostly city is covered in a midnight sky. Pitch black, not a single star or cloud. Not even the moon can be seen in the fragments of sky that peek out between the buildings.

Everything around me, just registering now. Trees, buildings, cars, people all high contrast black and white, and all covered in a star-less night sky.

Black and white. I am walking through a black and white city, full of black and white freaks.

I had the tremendous urge to have a drink. I wanted to find the nearest bum, grab his bottle and just run with it. Guzzling it down. Letting that putrid cheap burning flavor work its way down my throat and warm my stomach. That's just the beginning. Just the start of the process. The real experience hits a little while after the alcohol seeps into the blood stream. Rich molecules, carbon joined to hydrogen atoms. They fill my plasma and march with my my blood cells carrying oxygen and poison to my brain. It's a different state of mind when the chemical reaction occurs. Everything slows down, my thoughts, my movements, time. I stop carrying about everything. These hallucinations. Everything. My body keeps walking on it's own. Moving with the crowd. I know my eyes must be glazed over. I'm sure people are staring. I don't care. Fuck you. Fuck every single one of you. None of you give a shit about me.

You don't know my name or where I'm from. I'm starting to wonder myself. Even I don't care.

I'm joining all of you in the apathetic medicated mass of an existence. Fuck it all. We're pointless, a worthless species, every other Goddamn organism has a purpose, even the sonnava bitch dung beetle eats shit and serves it's existence as a decomposer. Algae produces oxygen, fucking bacteria converts energy all day and night, fuck you nature. Fuck you for making a Goddamn pointless species that does nothing but consume and waste and destroy the world around it. And fuck you mother and father and God and doctors for making me a part of it!

I marched with my fellow humans along the sidewalk. Our arms swinging and legs kicking forward to a silent militaristic beat. The alcohol, or something else, has taken full effect. Wait, I didn't drink any alcohol? My legs have taken on a life of their own. I tried to stand still but my legs kept moving forward with the crowd.

Suddenly dozens of beautiful women in fancy clothes paraded down the sidewalk around me, like my fellow side walkers and I had just gotten in the way of a herd. Some had their arms pinned back in an awkward pose like a straight jacket. Lips were stitched into smiles and I could swear I saw tears coming from the corners of their eyes. I watched as a gorgeous woman walked up to me, then right passed. I turned my head for one last glance expecting to see a beautiful ass following her, only to see a horrific anorexic back with a huge gash down her spine being held together with rough dark sutures. I walked passed another woman who had her nose burring in a compact mirror case like she was touching up her makeup. She glanced up at me as I passed and I realized she wasn't doing her makeup at all. She had a needle and thread pinched between her fingers and was busy sewing up a dark red laceration running along her cheek bone. Touching up her plastic surgery? The women were gone.

I looked at the bus benches, the alcoves, people leaning against walls. Everyone around me was engaged in some sort of twisted scenario. The cab drivers had on their gas masks, inhaling the car fumes. Naked beggars squatted on ledges of buildings like gargoyles, insects crawling all over their bodies and face. A suited man that looked like a city official giving a speech, a politician, was clawing at his throat trying to remove wads of filthy cash stuffed in his mouth. He stood atop a large set of granite steps behind a podium. A nest of news microphones attached to megaphones blasted a voice that obviously wasn't his, "Smile. Smile. Smile," it repeated. A large crowd of people stood with their backs to the politician and megaphones. Construction workers, high up on scaffolding, worked like Frankensteins. Using their power tools to cut and rip and assemble each other into freakish creations.

Everyone engaged in a freakish activity. I could spot old people along the ground naked with bulging rib cages. Their long boney spider vein covered limbs pushing them along the sidewalks, hands grasping medicine bottles. An incredibly fat kid was in an alley stuffing his face with candy. Not candy, I had only a second to glimpse what could only be tiny insect legs twitching through his clenched fist before he tossed whatever it was down his throat. Limos had wealthy types inside shoveling cash out the car windows to prevent from being smothered. An alley cat was nursing a hundred kittens. Literally, a hundred. A dog lay on the ground urinating on itself.

I wanted to gag.

Women, or transvestites, that could only be whores dressed in black stockings and garter belts. Black lipstick and nails. A look sexy enough for death. They clustered at street corners and down alleys covered in black brick. Some were on all fours on the street, bent over and getting fucked from behind. Fucked not from business men holding too much cash, lonely men or cheating husbands. But fucked by big black shadowy figures that looked like large dogs. Disgusting.

It was some sort of midnight freak show. A living ghost city. The vast majority of people on the sidewalks were business men and women marching like soldiers. We looked the same, pale faces sitting atop emaciated bodies dressed in black suits and skirts. Men and women looking like they just crawled out of the grave walked with dead serious stares. Eyes as black as their briefcases. Limp arms. They were white collared professionals in a comatose. A city full of them. They marched down the sidewalks, sat on the benches, hailed taxies, exited buildings. The more I walked, the more I took in and noticed more of these strange people I was becoming a part of. My quick reflection in a window. The greasy dumpster clothes I was wearing have been replaced with a suit just as black as theirs. How?

How is any of this possible? The city must be playing with my mind. How could these people be doing these things to themselves. Every face I saw was either holding back vomit or near passing out from pain. I'm almost certain I see tears building up in their eyes. My legs kept moving on their own. I felt my neck muscles stiffen. Slowly my head turned forward and locked in position, a dead stare straight ahead.

All I can do is roll my eyes around in their sockets. Peripheral vision picks up images, flashes of faces, all pale. It's not euphoric, yet I'm not scared. Just, accepting, I guess. Yeah, accepting. I'm shocked, yet unwillingly indifferent to everything going on around me. I've never experienced a state of mind like this before. Only drugs and dreams can explain something as bizarre as this. What am I drugged on? Why won't I wake up? Dementia. Insane. I must be going insane. So this is what its like when you become crazy. It must be schizophrenia.

As I let my body march down the street I stayed alert and took everything in. My eyes like cameras constantly receiving images. I try and read anything and everything quickly. Newspapers, store signs, billboards, anything. Maybe I'll find a clue to where I am. But the writing is even stranger than the visions. Newspaper headlines read, "Maybe I'll find a clue," and, "Why won't I wake up?". A billboard with giant writing states, "It must be schizophrenia." My thoughts, they are printed in massive text up above me and all around. Large photo advertisements hang in storefronts. Glossy family photos selling something. It's not the generic family you find in new picture frames or wallets. It's my family. Pictures of my family during the good years. Melanie and I smiling at each other. Our daughters first birthday. My family is in the ads. I'm confused and shock.

Someone is yelling up ahead. It's coming from a window up above me. Multiple voices now. I'm trying to make it out. A foreign language? No, I know this. It's not a melody but it's a verse. It's familiar. The Our Father? A prayer! They're yelling prayers. It's all garbled but I hear it. I'm not religious, never really was but I'm trying to focus on it. Almost comforting to hear something that should be positive and familiar. It's mixed up with other prayers. Too hard to make out and now it's fading behind me.

My legs take a sudden turn. I spin on a crack and my body walks right into one of the glossy skyscrapers. I'm inside, it's a lobby. Typical, modern and minimal. Black granite, black furnished sitting areas, high ceilings. Business suits are walking in every direction, but all organized like rows of dominos crisscrossing all over the place. Hard shoes on a hard surface sound the air above. Lighting classy and dim, but I see I'm in a row headed somewhere. We're checking into something I think. I see the back of the person's head in front of me. Clean cut, sharp suit. Can't see the shoes, but I'm guessing they're polished and black. Can't see his face, but I know it's pale and thin like the others. They all have face's that look sculpted out of white candle wax.

I hear the clang of glass. There's a bar. It's off to the side of the lobby and I'm straining my eyes to get a clearer look. Sexy. Super sexy business women. Black skirts, stockings. They probably have stitches holding their skin together somewhere. They're strapped to the bar stools, arms and legs, like mental patients ready for EST. Hair in a ponytails, tied down the back to the stool. Forcing them to point their heads straight up. Mouths gaping open in a silent yell. Male bartenders are pouring shots down their mouths, then taking shots themselves.

There's some sort of a queue going on here in the lobby. Many of us are sitting or standing in lines. I can't tell where they lead. All the black suits with tortured wax faces make a maze out of the lobby. My body advances with the line slowly now. My mind flashes back.

-SIX-

Only in a society this sick. This glutenous. This hyper sensitive. Can I say I am depressed. And sit, no lounge. With a cocktail. In front of a television. A full stomach. My health, in my thirties.

A machine. A zombie. A robot with a white collar, carpel tunnel and a 401k. Never did I imagine where my eleven by seventeen gold trimmed paper from the state university would take me: into a four by six foot cubicle for nine hours a day with a one hour lunch, 40 hours of vacation, holidays and weekends. Off to type meaningless reports. Well, I'm sure they meant something to someone. Hell, maybe the reports were super important and keep consumers satisfied, or countries from clashing. Or maybe they keep income up, expenses down and shareholders happy. Doesn't matter. At the end of the day I have a headache, numb wrists and need three drinks. I've put on three pounds a year steadily. Job satisfaction, drops every time my request for a raise, or a promotion gets declined.

Why am I still here? I ask myself that question all the time, and all the time I am reminded when my wife tells me it's bill week. Insurance and grocery costs are going up. The kids needs braces. I'm giving myself a headache just thinking about it.

I tried looking for a different job. But no one is going to offer me a role doing anything more than what I'm doing right now. I'm stuck, in a rut. A working nightmare.

And those were the good years at the job. The good thoughts. I should have known better than to complain back then. If I had known where my job was headed I would have savored those days, when my biggest complaint was no promotion and popping more Tylenol than I could jerk off to online porn.

Oh no, things got much worse. And to tell you the truth, it wasn't even because of Christina. Wish I could at least blame part of it on her. Well, maybe I could, towards the end at least.

Usually it works like this: you show up to a particular building every morning dressed in business appropriate clothes. A button down, slacks, clean underwear, maybe. You walk through the front door, small talk with the secretary. Find your floor, your section, your cubicle. Sit in the chair you've spent too much time trying to adjust to perfection. Log into your computer with one of a hundred passwords you have to keep stored in your head. Then wait. Wait for your computer to boot up. Wait for your emails to load, wait while you come up with responses that make you sound smart. Wait for your first tasks to be complete. Wait for first break, lunch, second break. Meetings. Phone calls. Training sessions.

Five o'clock. Wait. It's as bad as high school sometimes.

Your job has a title. a job description, your day-to-day duties. A pay grade. A team. Maybe a supervisor, the manger, their manager and so on until you reach the top. You think about making it up the ladder. What would it take. Is it worth it? Will it be more work, or less? A lot more pay, or just more hours?

And then your body starts the downward trend. You wake up after laying in bed for hopefully eight hours, sit at the breakfast table, sit in your car to work, sit at your desk, the lunch table, your desk, your car again, in front of the television eating dinner and of course fill in all the gaps with sitting on the toilet. You try to offset the effect all this sitting has on your skeleton by swinging weights around with your appendages at the gym, but it's never consistent. The sitting wins your body over.

I still can't decide what comes first, falling apart mentally or physically. Either way, you take this environment, these thoughts, and run them through your head everyday for years while your body sits there starring from one piece of glass and plate of food to the next. And you end up letting your life fly by. Time passes, years go by, pounds get added and you don't know where you're life went. The energy you had when you were younger. The drive, the motivation. The excitement and novelty of independence and contribution to the human race, all diminished. And you've let yourself go, mental and physically. You start slacking and it shows.

I started dressing sloppier. Little by little of course. Unclean clothes here and there. Maybe untuck the shirt a little earlier in the day. No belt one day, street clothes tee-shirt another day.

Sure enough, the self esteem started dropping. Come on man, do something. Do something with yourself. Is this as productive as you're ever going to get? Is this what you're going to be doing for the rest of your life? These reports are only good until I run the next batch. Even the Egyptian slaves who piled rocks contributed more to the human race. My job is worthless in the large scope of things. I am worthless.

And the quality of work dropped once again. It's a cycle.

So now I'm at the point where I'm coming into work more disheveled than I should be, my work has downgraded. My moral has plummeted. And I'm eating fried shit for lunch and fighting food comas with caffeine everyday.

Fuck.

And of course, the stuff with Christina started up and boosted my moral for a bit. Life was grand and things started improving. Quality went up because I was happy. I was fun to be around at work. I did my work and was happy about it. Because I had an outlet. Something was giving me happiness. And then, you know what happened with Christina, it all blew up in my face.

The announcement, the pressure, the threats. I was right back where I was a year ago, thinking the same worthless job thoughts. And the paranoia about the fetus growing inside Christina on top of that.

Fuck. Fuck.

"Did you hear?" My co-worker Willard's voice startled me. "Hey man, you sleeping again? I'd cut that shit out right now. At least till the smoke blows over."

"What are you talking about?" I looked down at my forearm. It had a big red spot where my forehead was pressing into it for the past, I

135

looked at my computers clock, forty minutes.

"Man, they're talking downsizing," Willard said.

"What do you mean?" I asked. Of course I knew what he meant. Why did I say that. I'm still sleepy.

"Milton just told me he went to lunch with George, and George told him they we're gonna start cutting our team," he said.

"What the fuck?"

"Yeah," Willard said, "They're gonna cut like twenty percent or some shit. That's like four of us. Something about automating these reports. They've got the dev's starting on it already."

"You're joking," I said. I looked him in the eyes. He was smiling. More like grinning, but it was a nervous grin. Damn, he's not joking. "Shit."

"Shits, right. Time to shit your pants," Willard groaned. He stared for a second, then, "Actually, maybe this is a good thing. You know I've been thinking about leaving for a while. At least this way I can cash in on unemployment for a while."

"Yeah, good for you," I said, "but I need this crappy job. You know Melanie doesn't do shit. And those kids suck up so much money."

He looked at me, a grin still, but with pitty eyes. "Shit sucks, man," and he walked away.

I'm going to get tacos for lunch. A lot of them.

Fuck. Fuck. Fuck.

A few days later, I'm thinking different thoughts. So do I approach my boss? Do I ramp up my quality? Come up with a new idea that'll give me points? Think! Think! I need this crappy job. That, or I need

Melanie to disappear, with the kids. Ok, I didn't think that. I take that back. At least the thing about the kids.

Think! I've got to come up with something before they make an announcement.

I've been popping more acetaminophen than usual the past few days. I need a new bottle.

"Here."

I looked up, Milton was standing at my cube entrance. He held out his hand with a couple pills in it and said, "I was just going to take these, but you look like you need them more than me."

I took the pills, "Tylenol? Pain killers?"

"No. Speed," he cracked a smile. He was joking. He always was.

"Hey," I said before he walked away, "so anymore news on that downsizing stuff, or what?" I swallowed the pills.

"I haven't heard anything. What about you?" he asked.

"No, nothing on my end," I said.

Willard rolled over, "You guys prepared for it?"

I just looked at him.

"Yeah, I bought a six pack and told my folks I'll be staying in the guest room for a while," Milton said half joking.

Willard leaned back in his chair, "I fixed up my resume last night. Put myself on a mission, a challenge. See if I can land a new job before they give me the announcement," he said. "That way I can give them the finger and not have to worry about it," he snickered and rolled away.

"Yeah well you better hurry," Milton said. "I heard they gave Eric her notice this morning. And you guys no she was gonna get it even if they didn't downsize." He started walking away, "thank God I'll never have to correct one her damn reports again."

I'm next. I know it. I'm going to throw up all that chow mein I ate.

Fuck. Fuck. Fuck. Fuck.

I needed a plan. Do absolutely nothing. No, I can't do that. Do something. I started scrambling, I was in a panic. I grabbed a note pad and started jotting down ideas. Things to make the company better. Marketing ideas, processes, flows to streamline reports, improve employee efficiency. It was all just a bunch of junk. Circles and lines all over the paper leading to nothing. I crossed out everything over and over. I had nothing.

For the next few days I went home sweating, stressed. I could barely get my work done. I was sick to my stomach all the time. Nauseous. I need a drink.

I'm going to get an ulcer. Is that even possible? I looked it up online. No. You can't get ulcers from stress. Then why am I shitting weird gooey stuff?

I'm not even eating full meals anymore. I need another drink.

I'm a wreck. I sit in my car in the parking lot, trying to cry, but just staring at my office building. The same stare I have when I get home at night and stare at my apartment for thirty minutes before going in.

What am I going to do? What can I do? Come on self-empowerment classes, lessons. I'm like an engine trying to turn over a positive thought. Nothing is happening.

My boss started having daily meetings. We had to report on the status of our tasks. We had to keep time logs. I spent two hours trying to write up my employee scorecard and company alignment goals. How the fuck more meaningful can I say I write reports that any computer program could probably do ten time faster. I can't.

I would stare at the reports. They looked like crosswords. I started drinking more coffee. Lots of water. I'd hold my water in to the point where I had to piss and then I'd drink even more water. I did it to take my mind off everything else around me. I thought about drugs. I couldn't afford them. I would stare at the objects on my desk and fantasize about ways I could kill myself with them.

I'm using every positive thought technique I can to keep my head above the shit line. But it's getting harder and harder. I keep dipping under and getting mouthfuls of shit. I'm nearly choking on it. Everyday is a constant struggle.

I have to take one task at a time. Have to keep a smile on my face.

I retreat to the bathroom more than usual. I just sit in the stall on the toilet. Not even using it, just sitting there with my pants up staring at the back of the stall door. Almost meditating. But pretty much daydreaming. I don't even masturbate.

It's funny how when things turn to shit in life, they turn to shit fast. It's not like everything else stays constant, or stable and you lose your job. No. You lost your job, get your mistress pregnant. Get two parking tickets. Break you stereo. Catch your dick in your zipper. And your stress levels go up, this in turn causes GI track problems. The stress brings a host of problems. Muscle cramps. Headaches come regularly. Pains everywhere. Symptoms for everything on the web. Hypochondria sets in. Thoughts of health insurance expiring. You worry more, you stress more. The cycle gets worse. You can't sleep at night, your immune system gets weak. You lose your appetite, sure I'm losing weight, but I feel weak. Cancer? My hairs coming out. My short term memory is going. I lost my wallet. Mentally I'm a runaway train on the verge of a panic attack. I'm not thinking clearly, I'm making bad decisions and putting the wrong gas in my car at the pump. I'm panicking. Getting speeding tickets because I'm not paying attention. Need to go to traffic school to keep this off my insurance. Just another thing on the to-do list. I'm spending money on things I shouldn't. Staring at the television, not even watching it anymore. I'm in a tailspin. I'm losing control of my life. My friends, if I can call them that, don't understand, because I don't tell them. I don't want to drag people down so I mention as little as possible. Can't talk to my wife about shit. We'll just end up fighting about my job, and how the fuck could I ever explain the mistress thing.

Im stuck. I'm stuck. Therapy? Counseling?

I tried a few sessions. Pointless. I could have gotten the same advice off a website. My therapist was hot, and any other time in life I would have used her as jerk off material. Right now, I have no, absolutely no, sex drive.

I wish I was dead.

And that's how it happened. Those magic words led to me where I am today. I thought it again. I wish I was dead. The first thing I've thought that felt anything but bad, in I don't know how long. I sat in my car staring at my workplace and thought the thoughts again. I wish I was dead. And again, I wish I was dead.

I had a one track mind, and I kept the thoughts running all morning. I let my body do it's thing, walking into work. Past Christina without a word. It was on autopilot. I was used to this. The whole time I repeat 'I wish I was dead' like a mantra. 'Om, I wish I was dead'.

It got me through that work day a lot easier. I tired it at home. At the dinner table, watching, no staring at the television. Showering, brushing my teeth, laying in bed next to Melanie. I even fell asleep. Four hours of sleep, an improvement.

I was now living to think this thought. And just like anything else, I built up a tolerance to it. 'I wish I was dead' wasn't good enough after a while. I started adding ways. Methods.

I would sit behind the wheel of my car and look for ideal places on the way to work to swerve off the road, or into an oncoming car. What's better, hanging myself, poison, slit wrists? What's easiest? Antifreeze over a long period, bleach and ammonia in a bucket? I would fantasize about picking up a gun. Blowing my brains out in different places. What would be better, in front of the wife and kids? At the dinner table? Before or after the meal? Depends on the meal I guess. At work? In my car in the parking lot? Will life insurance pay anything? Why do I care? Should I care? Is that bad that I don't care about what happens to my family after I'm gone? Did I used to care about this?

What would it be like dying? Would I feel anything? For how long? How would people react? My family? Christina? My coworkers? My boss? I imagined them at my funeral. The thoughts were endless. Before I knew it the day was over and I was ready for bed.

But a tolerance grew. I needed more. Christina was pushing harder. Melanie was nagging more. The thought out of me being next to lose my job at work was too intense. I had to do it. I had to. I had to end my life. Suicide was the only answer. But I didn't want to. I didn't really want to die. I don't think I do. I don't know if it was fear or something else. But I couldn't kill myself, I had to think of an alternative. I just needed to disappear and make everyone else forget about me. Then I could start life over again. Without a wife, a pregnant mistress, a dead-end job.

When you get this low in life. You barely exist. You're a blank face. You stare a lot. A lot. There's nothing to say. And even if there was, you're too depressed to say it. Just a shell. You just roll your eyes around and stare at everything, at nothing. You're body and limbs are too heavy to move. What's the point of walking to the water cooler, copier, the kitchen, the yard. You want to cry, you try. Key word is want, but you can't. It's taking more effort than you thought. You're stomach has the worst butterflies you've ever experienced. It's like you have an ulcer or something. you're completely nauseous and want to throw up. Mornings are terrible. Especially weekends, when there's no reason to really get up.

I'm depressed.

I don't want counseling. I don't care.

I've never been laid off. But you can feel it. When it's close. I mean sure, people in my team we're talking about it all the time. But I've been getting this feeling. I know it's close. I look at myself in the mirror, before work. During work. I see myself. I know what I look like. My attitude. The quality of my work. I'm trying, I'm really trying to shape up, but I can't do it. Everyday I get worse and worse. Sometimes I think I want to get laid off.

Why would I want that? I don't know. Some sort of sick self-sabotage. but I don't have any other explanation except I am severely depressed.

I'm not really doing my work anymore. I having a hard time seeing the point. I know people are looking at me when they pass my cubicle. Talking about me behind my back. I see how awkward they get when I walk in the break room.

"Hey," it was Milton. Even Milton has been acting weird around me. No one wants to be near me cause it probably looks bad for them. "Rick wants to see you."

My heart quickened. Oh great, the boss wanted to see me. "Alright," I said. I stood up and started walking to his office.

Milton just watched me walk away. I know he probably had a sorry look on his face. I could feel my hands getting sweaty, my face hot. I know what's going on. What to expect. Why am I nervous? I walked, but I felt stiff. Everything seemed quiet to me. I could tell people were looking at me as I walked passed. Willard's cubicle, Eric's, Winnie's. I should have been in the bathroom. I wish I had more coffee in me, then I could focus on having to pee.

I walked slower.

Relax, relax. You need this job. Your subconscious may be setting you up for failure. Or you may just be stressed and depressed, but you need this job. Why do I need this job? To put food on the table and pay the bills. To pay for your kids. Cause your wife won't. Those aren't good reasons. Yes they are. I battled with myself while I walked.

I was about halfway to his office when I decide to stop in the bathroom first. Ok, ok think this out. Don't just rush in, go to bathroom for a minute and pull yourself together.

I walked into the small restroom, ok good, it's empty. I chose a stall, closed the door and sat alone in the small space. It was quiet. I never thought about it, but the stall was just like my cubicle. A small private box. Mine, temporarily. Just like my cubicle. I'll probably walk into the bosses office, get the speech and have to turn my cubicle back over in a couple weeks.

Breath. I breathed. Calm down. I didn't calm down. I stared at my hands. They were shaking. Do something, pull yourself together. Think yourself down. I feel malnourished. I started unwinding toilet paper, not really sure of why I was doing it. Once I had a ball of it, I just squeezed it. I leaned forward and buried my face in my hands. The toilet paper was sort of soft. I bit into it. It hurt my jaw and I bit harder.

Think suicide thoughts. You need them.

Ok, gun. Thought it. Rope, that too. I need something new right now. Something extreme. Something here in the bathroom. Get creative. I kept my head buried in the toilet paper in my hands.

Someone walked in. I listened as the guy walked to one of the urinals and peed. I could visualize the whole thing. He didn't flush, but he washed his hands. The blow drier went on and I heard him open and close the door. The blow drier stay on. I listened to the white noise. It felt good. Soothing. I don't want it to stop. Ever. I don't want to leave this bathroom stall.

I thought of the blow drier. Electric. I imagined sticking my hands in the vent. Could I get electrocuted? What if I put water in there. If I got a mouthful of water and sprayed it out of my mouth and into the drier. What if I peed in it. Hit my head on it over and over again. Was there something sharp I could cut myself with? Could I suffocate with it?

The thoughts distracted me. Calmed me.

My hands were still shaking, but not as bad. I stood up. I walked out of the stall and pressed the hand drier button to turn it on. The comforting white noise. I listened to it while I stared in the mirror. My hair was greasy, uncut, ruffled. I ran my fingers through it and tried to straighten it. Hairs came off my scalp and stayed between my fingers. I did it again and more hairs came out. Again. I rinsed my mouth out. Turned the blow drier on again. Tried to straighten my shirt, it's too big for me now. I'm losing weight, but not for a good reason. My belt is as tight as it will go and my pants still sag a little. I can't do anything about my unshaven face. I try to pop a zit, it just makes my skin red. I hit the blow drier again. I'm so pale. I look old. I look beat up. Worn out. I haven't stared at myself in the mirror for this long in a while. I wash my hands. I lean forward and inspect my teeth. Cup my hands over my mouth and try to smell my breath.

The bathroom door opens and Milton walks in. I start washing my hands again, like I'm just wrapping up in here.

Milton looks at the blow drier, then me.

"What did the boss say?" he asks.

"Haven't seen him yet, going there now," I said.

He looked confused.

I finished washing, held my hands under the drier for a few seconds, not long enough to dry them, and walked out. I walked quickly. Don't think. Don't think. Just react. No, just move. Like a robot, an insect.

Rick's door was closed. I looked through the little window in the door and saw he was on his computer. He saw me and motioned for me to come in.

I walked into my boss's office. It's just like one the cubicles, only

145

bigger. Yeah, it's got windows, a bigger desk, a little row of chairs in front of the desk. Nothing I ever thought about making my own. I've never had the ambition, aspiration to get to his place. I was uncomfortably comfortable in my own cubicle.

"You wanted to see me?" I said. Asked.

"Yeah, have a seat," he said focused on something on the computer. "Close the door."

I was going to do that anyway. I know this won't be good. Don't think that, stay as presentable as you can.

I took one of the seats in front of his desk.

Harry is a big guy. He spills out of his chair. Always looks like he's going to break it. He's got one of those faces that make you wonder if he's either analyzing you or thinking about something else entirely. Probably analyzing, he's a smart guy.

He finishes up on the computer. His chair spins so he can face me. I know he doesn't want to look at me. Or maybe it's just that I don't want to look at him.

I force myself and squeeze my thigh. I think he can see my hands, oh well. Squeeze harder.

"What's going on?"

"Nothing," why did I say that? "What do you mean?"

"Is everything ok with you? I know this layoff thing is shaking a lot of fellows up. Is that what this is?" he asked, his voice was actually sincere.

"Yes, honestly, I'm stressing a bit over it," he looked at me as if there was more. "Other stuff too. I'm stressing out over other stuff also."

"Like what?"

What do I say? "Just home stuff. Family." I'm talking, ok this is a good thing.

"You know, we on track for being friends when you started here," he almost sounded sad. I think it was more pity though. "We went out a few times on the weekends I remember, fishing and happy hours."

My eyes started shifting downward.

"You were a lot different back then. More eager, enthusiastic," he paused, "It showed in your attitude." I think he was searching for things to say. Small compliments. "What happened?"

What am I supposed to say?

"What's going on? I know the job isn't the greatest, most interesting thing. But still, what's happened to you over the years? I've watched you fall apart slowly, the past couple years seem to have really hit you."

I opened my mouth, I don't know what I was going to say. He watched. Waited, but nothing came out.

I closed it.

"Jesus!" his voice had a restrained frustration. He was a good manager, I have to admit. He was always staying calm, even when things were turning ugly in the office. Always stuck up for us, looked out for us. A good guy to work for. But right now, now I could see he was torn, he was fidgeting with stuff and agitated. "I'm doing the best I can here. You know what's going on here. Why aren't you turning around? Shaping up?" He was talking faster now, "You know, it's out of my control. I've got to be honest. They want me to let one more go," talking really fast, "they want me to let you go. I don't have to give you this heads up. But the pressures on. They wanted me to let you go today." the first pause. "I don't want to have to do this."

He looked at me.

I looked at him.

I looked away.

I couldn't say anything. I couldn't breath.

"Well, what am I supposed to do? I don't have a choice, and you're not helping."

I looked down.

I should say something. I need to say something. Why am I not fighting for this job? Is it because I feel like there's nothing I can do? Is it because I don't have the energy, the ambition, the drive? Or is it because I laid awake all night last night, in a bed next to a woman who doesn't think anything of me, while I thought about that other woman in my life that thinks even less of me. I haven't had solid sleep in ages.

I know this is hard for him. I seriously appreciate everything he is doing for me. I just can't seem to say it. I can't speak. Restrained by my own emotional turmoil.

"You know," he started up again. And now he's looking away. "You know, maybe this," he's talking slow and choosing his words careful I can tell. "Maybe this will be good for you. Maybe this job just isn't right for you right now. Maybe you need more than just a two week vacation."

I wasn't responding, so he stopped.

I remember leaving his office not knowing what hit me. Like I was in a movie the whole time. I wanted to go back in time and say something. Act different. But at the same time, I knew that even if I could go back in time, it would have ended up the same. What is wrong with me? I know the answer to that question, but I can't help but ask it right now.

I have just destroyed this job for myself. My family. What am I going to do? How am I going to tell my wife about this. The boss gave me a few more days until he has to officially let me go. I appreciated it, but what am I supposed to do in a few days.

I can't turn around. I know I wont be able to fight to keep up this job. He can see right through me. Everyone can. I wear my emotions on my stained, untucked shirt.

I'm going to sit at my desk and stare. That's all I can do right now.

I'm doing everything I can to get through the workday. Still drinking as much coffee and tea as I can hold without pissing my pants. I heard it was bad for my prostate, I'm ok with that. Really helps to keep my mind off everything. I'm walking to the break room to get a refill. I've decided to stick with tea today. Every time I get up to refile my glass, I just add a brand new tea bag instead of just re-using the bag and refilling the cup with hot water. I've got four tea bags in my cup already. And of course, as I'm walking and staring down at my cup thinking just how many bags I can fit in there, the suicide thoughts float in.

I wonder. I wonder if you can kill yourself with tea. A tea overdose? Is it possible? Are there chemicals in tea that taken in large quantities could kill you? I need to look this up. I wonder if I could fit an entire box of tea bags in here, that's what, twenty or so bags? I could let the whole thing seep for thirty minutes. Then, then just sip it. No swig it. No sip, and maybe something would happen. Yeah, I'd probably get sick to my stomach, or nauseous. But I'm already nauseous and sick. Maybe it would just destroy my kidneys.

"You're really starting to look like shit you know that."

Her voice cut right into my fantasy. I had just walked in on Christina in the break room. I didn't even respond. I don't have the energy. She gave a smug sigh and started pouring herself coffee.

"If I were you, I'd shape up. We all know what's going on around here. What's probably going to happen, with the lay offs. "I'm due in a matter of weeks, and you know what happens then if I don't get what I want." She stared at me and I didn't respond. "You know people are talking about you."

I stared at the tea boxes, thinking of which, if any was most likely to contain chemicals.

"And don't think I'm going to feel sorry for you."

Black tea probably, it's more processed, right?

"I was actually just going to go drop something off at your desk," she said. She placed a folded up piece of paper on the counter next to me. I looked at it.

"Read it," she said staring at me. I hate it when she stares at me.

I unfolded the paper. It was a short note:

"Hello. We've never met, but I'm pregnant with your husband's daughter. He couldn't stop sticking that short circumcised dick with the mole by his nut sack in me."

There was an illustration of a waist, with a short dick, and a happy face mole on one of the thighs where my real life mole is.

What is wrong with this girl? Is she seriously nuts?

"What do you think? Think she'll like it, your wife?" she said. I was still staring at the note but could tell she was smiling.

I just stay quiet. All I could do was stare at the boxes of tea. I need to get out of here. I can't work with this going on. I need to get out of this room. I need suicide thoughts right now. I went back to the tea thoughts, imagining myself eating the tea leaves.

"I'm feeling like you're not getting the message. Don't make me do something I don't want to," she said calmly. "You know what I want."

"Why are you doing this to me? Can't you see my life is turning to shit? I have nothing, nothing to give you. I have no money. I'm in debt as it is," I begged. "I'm probably going to be unemployed in a month," my voice was panicky, but I know she didn't care.

"You're a pussy!" she hissed.

"What? Why am I a pussy?"

"Because you got a woman pregnant and you can't live up to your cock. You're not responsible you fuck. You're going to have a hell of a time explaining it to the court."

"Please, please!" my voice was getting dry and weak. My whole body was falling apart. "I'm begging you, I'll do anything. I can't handle this in my life right now. Believe me. Believe. If I had the money I would give it to you. I have nothing. Please don't," I could barely speak, "don't have this baby!" I'm choking on the words. I'm trying hard not to throw up.

"It's too late for that. You know that," no empathy in her voice.

I felt my eyes getting watery.

"Well give it up for adoption," the words barely came out a whisper.

"What's that?" she said. "Give it up for adoption? My own child?"

I could barely breath. Think suicide thoughts faster. I bet there's no chemicals in tea. Drinking this stuff is probably making me healthier. Wrong direction, think suicide. I'd be more likely to die from tea if I tried to slit my wrist with these little staples holding the bags together. Faster. Or strangling myself with these two inch strings, or suffocating on the

151

paper envelops. Or microwaving the staples with my face right in front of the microwave window. It helps, her voice gets drained out.

I turn and stare at her. She's leaning against the microwave table. We fucked on that table once, sort of. Yeah, it was after hours one day. She was wearing very tight pants, I remember that. She was in a completely different pose than the one she's in now. It could have even been the moment she got pregnant. I can't think of this, it's making me sicker.

"look, if you don't," her face was getting stern, "there's gonna be shit to," her voice was low but definitely strong. "Are you even listening to me?"

I'm miles away in my head. Caught in a fantasy, it's all I can do to get through this encounter. I'm imagining myself laying on the floor of the break room. My eyes staring up at the ceiling, but there's no life behind them anymore. My coffee cup, broken on the floor next to me. And tea all over the floor. Gallons of tea. My body is floating in a sea of black tea that's overflowing the small generic room. I've drank more liquid than humanly possible and it's ruptured everything organ I own. Especially my bladder.

I'm not listening to a word she's saying.

But I hear her voice when she stands up, flings her cup of coffee on me says, "You're scum! You're shit! You know that. Pathetic!"

The coffee was scolding and I jumped, but I didn't rush to wash it off with cold water. She walked out of the room pissed. Pissed at me, when I was the one that just got burning liquid poured on me. I looked down at my dirty button down white shirt. A big brown splatter. I made it look like blood with my imagination.

Why? Why should I go back to my desk? Why should I try to keep my job? Family, what's the purpose of all this? Life? Survive? Reproduce? No, as a species we're passed that. We make our own purpose.

I keep the tea death fantasy's going for the rest of the workday.

I can't take this. Why am I here. Why am I doing this to myself? Why? Why, why? I know this isn't the best time for self exploration and philosophies. But honestly, why am I here? Existing? And why at this job? How is my life being useful, contributing to the human race? Is this the best I can do? Even if I was happy, and my marriage was going semi-smoothly, what would I be doing? Working here to pay bills, and use the extra money, if there was any, on vacations. Subjecting myself to the same monotonous activity nine hours a day. Nothing will ever change. If I would have been able to keep this job, was I supposed to work here till I was an old man? Doing this same lousy work?

I had entered one track mind territory. I ran the same thoughts and questions over in my head for the rest of the afternoon and while I drove home. I pretty much entered a race with my thinking. I ran a red light and missed one of my turns. A turn I've been doing twice a day for over ten years, but won't be doing anymore. Say goodbye to this commute.

The world doesn't work the way you think it does when you're younger. Friends are not easy to make and keep. People don't get married to their dream girls. You don't get along with your kids and understand them. You don't always end up doing what you dreamed you would do when you were four feet tall. Businesses are as corrupt as politicians. Everything at work is fake. The relationships, the small talk. You spend half your time, and possibly your life with these people, yet you never really connect with them. Pretty much everything in life turns to shit. First your youth dies, then your parents die and leave you here. Stranded, in time with all these strangers and this strange life and a memory of a happy innocent childhood that only makes you depressed to recall.

I drove home calm. Calmer than I should have been. It wasn't sudden, or maybe it was. But all my anxiety, all my nervousness disappeared. I don't know if I'd say I was peaceful, but I definitely felt relaxed. In a good strange way. Maybe it was a helpless feeling, an acceptance of losing control over everything going on around me. I found myself driving slowly.

I was looking out my windshield, staring straight ahead and avoiding obstacles, but I wasn't looking at anything. It was as if I was on autopilot, letting my body drive the car home while my mind got comfortable and relaxed with my newfound state. Road hypnosis. I didn't care. Indifferent. Apathetic. Lost. Helpless. Devastated. Destroyed beyond repair. I had finally given up. My nerves finally called it quits. Neurons and nerve endings alike. I didn't want to beg Christina anymore. didn't care about fighting for my job. Didn't have anything left in me to give.

I didn't even care, or need to fantasize about suicide to get home.

I knew what I had to do. Knew there was only one solution. One way out of this mess.

Giving up completely. I couldn't solve my problems, so I just needed to leave them.

I had to get out of here. I had to disappear. Had to abandon everything, jump ship.

And there was only one way I could do this.

At the same moment I thought of the solution, I drove right past where I could execute this solution. It hit me all at once. I had to fake my death, and I would use this bridge that I drive over everyday on my commute.

Sixty, seventy feet high above the lake.

Oh my God that's it! I thought it again. I had to fake my death. Fake my death! Instantly I got a rush. Excited.

I had to fake my death, and I had to do it soon. This was the solution. This was the way out of this mess of a life. The only way out. I could use this bridge, it was perfect. People were known to have killed themselves on this bridge, it wasn't common, but common enough.

I had to plan this.

For the first time since I started fucking Melanie I was excited about something. I fantasized and planned all the way home. Even when I got home I sat in the car and kept thinking. I went inside, said hello, and went straight to the bathroom.

The kind of intense thinking where your face is just in a dead stare, but your brain cells are working a million miles an hour to process an idea. An idea that will change everything, a solution. The only solution.

Inside the bathroom, on the toilet. Kept thinking. How was I going to pull this off. How am I going to do this? Do they need to find a body to believe I died. Is it possible, is there a way to do this without a body?

I'll be free.

What about just part of a body? Could I do it, leave a part of me? Like my hand? Or just a finger, or a toe? A tooth? How would that work? What if I just left an article of clothing, a personal belonging and a note?

No more Melanie.

Can I drive my car off the bridge? Is that enough? Blood, blood, if I leave a trail of blood? Skin cells, everything is DNA now. Saliva, body fluids.

No more Christina. No more kids. Oh God, the kids.

Think. Think! I need to do this tonight. I can't deal with this one more day. I don't care if I'm being emotional, I need to do this and get it over with.

Ok, think of other deaths. Stories you've heard of the bridge, people you know. Movies, television shows. How is it done? Ok, there's always a news story. So and so was found this morning. They were reported missing at night, history of depression, suicide attempts. We found the body this morning in the lake. They left a note. Toxicology report is pending, investigation underway, no suspects. We suspect suicide but it hasn't been confirmed.

Ok, that's me. That's what I need. They have a body, I can't give them that. What can I give them. Suspicion. Maybe not a history of depression, but I can give them a history of 'something was wrong for a while'. I've never tried to kill myself, but I've definitely been out late and disappearing for a while at night because of Christina. Ok, we're getting somewhere.

Things weren't perfect at home, there was trouble, fights.

There was a knock on the door. Loud. I waited.

"Yes?" I said.

"What's going on?" it was Melanie. "You've been in there a while, everything ok?"

Perfect. That's right, I didn't say anything when I came home. I just ran straight to the bathroom and ignored everyone. "Yes, no," shit. "Yes," what the fuck do I say?

"What?" Melanie said. I couldn't tell if she was annoyed or just confused. Probably both.

"I'm, I'm," I don't know. "I don't know?" Honest. Honest is good. I don't even have to fake anything.

"Want to open the door?" her voice softened. A little.

"Ok," I said it. But I didn't do anything. I'll be free.

"Want to open the door?" she said again.

"Ok," I put my hand on the knob. I know she could hear it. She was being nice.

We both waited, and finally I turned the knob. It took her to push the door open though.

It was perfect. She saw me sitting on the toilet. The lid was closed of course, and I was fully clothed. Shirt, pants all disheveled. My shoes were off. Hunched over, a towel in my hands. I'm sure my face had 'depressed' written all over it. My eyes must have said 'I feel worse than shit', if not, my mind definitely did.

"What? What are you doing in here?"

"I'm not feeling good."

"What are you, sick?"

"No," not like that.

157

She sat down on the edge of the tub and tried to face me in the small bathroom. It was fifty fifty with her. I didn't know if she would snap and go off on me acting like a weirdo, or if she'd take some sort of sympathy and care about what I was going through. Years ago she would have supported me through anything. Now, she just got turned off and impatient with me anytime it looked like I was having a bad day.

This was worse than a bad day. This had become a bad life. Maybe she'll be different right now.

"Want to talk?" she asked, even though she had already made herself comfortable staring at me like one of our children. Our children, hard to imagine I have offspring with this woman. I bet she's just curious, that's all. She doesn't really care how I feel.

"Sure," I said. I have to try and stay open minded. At least she's going halfway, I could do the same.

"So..." she said.

"Well," ok I need to say the right things. Maybe not the right things, but I need to get the message across that things aren't going well. I'm at wits end. I'm depressed. I'm capable of anything, but she has no real reason to worry. What am I thinking. I just have to be honest. I'm not faking anything. I fucking hate my life. "Well, I don't know where to start."

"Why don't you start with why you're sitting in the bathroom."

"I think I'm close to having a breakdown. I think," there. That was good. I think.

"Why?"

"I don't know. Everything is going wrong."

"What's everything?"

Jesus, she was on top of every question. "Everything. My job, my stress levels. Us. You know, you see it all." Yeah, she should know. She sees me come home from work every day. Stressed out, quiet, withdrawn. She must know I'm laying awake in bed next to her at night. I know she knows we don't have sex. I can't even remember the last time.

"What's going on at work?"

How do I answer this. I seriously don't need a fight right now. Last thing I want is to argue about money. Or maybe I do? I need a minute to think. I don't have a minute.

"There's a lot of pressure. We lost some people," ok it's better to say less. Don't tell her I'm going to lose my job. Once it's out there I can never take it back. She'll find out anyway, sooner or later.

"What do you mean, you 'lost' some people?" her voice was calm.

"A couple guys quit about the same time, so we have more of a workload than usual," ok I'm doing good.

"Ok, but everyone else is in the same boat, right?"

"True, and we're all stressing," no I shouldn't have said that. My stress is worse. "I guess I'm just getting the worse end of the stick."

"I'm sorry," she sounded genuine. "Is there anything you can do? Tell Rick your boss?"

"We talked," honest, "he's got a solution," honest again. Yeah, he's going to lay me off. Don't say that though.

"Well, that's good. Right?"

"Yeah, I guess."

"So what else is bothering you. Come on. I've seen you handle stress at work before. It doesn't usually affect you this bad."

I think she's avoiding the 'us'. "Like I said, us. Family life." Please don't get defensive, please don't get defensive. I can't handle that right now.

She stayed quiet.

I stayed quiet.

We looked at each other.

She put her hand on my knee. This was odd.

Did she think I was thinking divorce?

We stared at each other. I'm not sure of what is going through her mind, but I can guess. She's either thinking I'm nuts and she's got to get the hell away from me soon before I have a break down and she has to take care of me, maybe live with her mother, or, or. Or she's remembering. Remembering who she married. Who I am. What we used to be.

I stared at her eyes. Into her eyes. I loved you Christina. I loved you so much, at one time.

I could almost feel her eyes saying it back to me.

There was a time when you were my angel and I would have done anything for you. I remember meeting you. How you changed my life. My outlook on everything, relationships. Someone I could picture myself with. Marrying and getting old together. I never thought any girl would be right for me and then you came along. I was young. You were young. We had the whole world and life ahead of us. Inseparable. We talked about marriage, having a house, kids. I told you, you could be a stay at home mom. I'd take care of you, give you everything you wanted. You listened to everything I had to say, gave me support through school and the start of my career.

I'm staring at her, and remembering the good days. The beginning.

I'm trying to remember the things we had in common, but I'm struggling. We liked the same music, sort of. We enjoyed going out. We went to the same school, university. Our friends didn't really mesh well, but that was ok. We didn't have the same interest in studies, that was ok too. We didn't really want the same things out of life, or have a similar history. Jesus, it didn't matter. We got along, we needed each other. At the time. Back then. Now, now I feel like I'm living with a stranger. Sleeping in the same bed with a different woman. I'm sure she feels the same. What happened to us?

I opened my mouth to say 'I love you', but nothing came out.

"What happened to us?"

She shook her head, "I don't know?"

My eyes started tearing up. She could see it.

I wanted to lean forward and kiss her. I couldn't do it. It felt too strange.

Timothy started crying from the living room.

"I'll put the kids to bed early, " she said, "then you and I can keep talking uninterrupted." She got up. "Why don't you take a shower and try to relax."

She closed the door and left me alone in the bathroom.

I think I will take a shower. My last shower here. I have to stay focused. I have a goal now. Probably the first goal I've had in ages. I need to get out of here. Tonight. I'm not spending one more morning in this apartment.

My stomach started turning.

Fifteen, twenty, thirty minuets later? I don't know. All I know is I threw up coffee in shower, cried a lot finally, scrubbed my skin till I had a first degree burn on my chest, figured out a plan to fake my death, threw up again, dried off, brushed my teeth, revised my plan, put lotion on my face, stared at myself in the mirror, drank water out of the sink, stared at myself again, stared deeper, tried to see past my pupils, tried to imagine these eyes when I was ten years old, cried a little more, tried to make the redness go away, realized it would help my case, left the redness alone.

She was waiting for me in the bedroom. the lights were dimmed. We never dimmed the lights anymore. I think she was trying to set a mood.

She was laying in bed under the covers. Watching me. Honestly, this is the woman I date for a year before marrying, we fucked our brains out when we started going out. We did the dirtiest things on our honeymoon. We have two kids together. I've stuck my dick in her countless times. But everything is different now. It died long ago. I stared at her in the bed and didn't know what to do. I don't look at her the same anymore. I know she felt it too.

She went out on a limb to do this for me. For us? I had to try. I'm not breaking my plan. I'm still going through with this. I'm glad the lights are dimmed at least, hopefully she'll pick up that I've been crying. I walked over to the bed and let my towel fall off before I climbed under the covers with her.

It was awkward.

I tried kissing her. Passionless. It felt like how it should. Two mouths rubbing against each other. Forced.

I pulled the covers away and tried kissing her neck and breast. She just laid there, silent.

Her body felt strange. I half wanted her to get turned on, and half didn't care. I tried going down on her, it helped a little. I tried sticking my half hard dick inside my wife. Within a minute I was totally limp. It was pathetic. She was embarrassed. I was even worse. I rolled off of her and we just laid there staring at the ceiling, silent. God, this is so awkward. I wish we didn't even try.

She rolled over so her back was to me. I don't know if she's crying softly, or completely disgusted.

I can't take this. I have to get out of here. This is the time. This is it. Ride the emotions. I'm sick as shit. I want to throw up again, but there's nothing in me. Nauseous.

Get out of bed. Get out of this bed, right now. Do it!

I got out of the bed.

"Where are you going?"

"I'm sorry, I have to go think," I said putting half my clothes on.

"Where?" she was hurt and annoyed. I have to get out of here, quick.

"I'm just going to go outside."

"What do you mean? Where are you going?"

"Nowhere, I'm just going go outside and think. I don't feel good."

"Well I don't feel good either. Stay here. Talk to me," she started sitting up in bed like she might get out.

"No, you don't have to get up. I'll be back. I'm just going to go for a short walk," what is she doing? Don't get up. Don't follow me. "I'll be back soon. I just need a few minutes." Oh crap, I've got to get out of here.

I grabbed my shoes and belt and left the room without looking back.

Did I really just do that? Is that really how I just left my wife? I

163

thought about going back inside the bedroom and kissing her goodbye. I didn't, I can't. But I'm never going to see her again. Don't go back.

I walked down the hall, past the kids rooms. They were probably asleep by now. I thought about sticking my head in their rooms. I can't. I can't. I need to stay focused. I'll break down if I do. I might not go through with it. Just keep walking.

I put my belt on while I walked. Stopped in the kitchen to dig up a pen and paper. I grabbed the plastic gallon of generic store brand rum from off the fridge before I opened the front door quietly. I knew she knew I was going to leave, but I wanted to do it silently anyway.

I was still putting pieces of the plan together as I stood outside the apartment. Talk about last minute planning. We have a cheap little shed. It's one of those out-of-box sheds you store your lawnmower and other yard junk in. I also have an old bike in there. Sure enough, the tires are flat and its filthy. That's ok. I haven't used it in years. It will still work, maybe? No one will ever know it was missing. I managed to get the bike in the backseat of the car. Then I got in the drivers seat.

Hard to believe it was less than ten minutes ago I was inside my wife, freaking out. And now I'm sitting behind the wheel of my car. Staring at our place. I'll never see them again, or this place. Five minutes and everything is over. Her eyes, my kids rooms, that kitchen, the television, everything we bought together. All the fights, this strange environment. This dwelling we made. All the good intentions and the reality of it. A complete disappointment, a waste. A wasted life.

They'll be ok. She'll go to her mothers. She has a sister, a support group. The kids will be fine. Probably better off. I can't stay here long. She won't come out, but the longer I wait, the more I might get cold feet.

I need to keep moving forward. This is the new me, I am going to keep moving. No stopping.

I turned the engine, put my life in reverse. Pulled out of the drive and shifted my outlook forward. I started driving back to the bridge, slowly, letting my newfound fantasy of faking my death and new life fuel me.

Everything was dark. Even though I'm close to the suburbs, this bridge is far enough away it doesn't get much light. There's some lights on the bridge itself, but they only light the pavement below. Other than that, it's just me, the light of the moon, my car that is long overdue at the shop for many, many things, this bottle of booze and a notepad.

It took me a little while to find, but after crossing the bridge a few times I finally scoped out a spot where I could pull the car off and observe the bridge and traffic without being seen easily.

Ok, let's think about this. I was shaking. Excited, nervous. Of course I had never done anything like this before. Never even thought I would. Ok, so what's the plan? What's the plan, huh?

I laughed aloud. "What's the plan, eh?" I asked myself. I looked down at the bottle of rum. It was big, a ridiculous size. Full of cheep booze. Could I do this? Am I really doing this? I honestly don't have a plan. I just thought if I could get out here, away from everything, and stare at the bridge and my intentions in the face, it would come to me.

Well. I am a man at wits end. I have nothing. I have nowhere to go. For support, for comfort. Ok, maybe that's a lie after what I just experienced with my wife. But who knows how long that would last. It was fake. Forced, unnatural.

165

I looked at the bottle of booze. I hadn't planned on drinking it. I grabbed it at the last second thinking it would be a good prop, or item to have handy. I think I was thinking, well I was thinking a couple things. Guy gets drunk and jumps off bridge, or guy gets drunk and drives off bridge. Of course jumping is easier to pull off, but I think the driving would be more believable.

I tried having a moment. Tried to reflect on my life and everything I've been going through. Was this the best solution. I've already decided, stick to it.

A car drove by. They couldn't see me. I was hidden pretty well. But if a cop drove by, and he was looking he would see me for sure. I don't know how long I should wait. I need to do this, I need to figure this out. I looked at the booze.

Ok. Go.

I wasn't going to do it, but I opened the booze. Strong smell. Shit. No chaser. No mixer. I looked in my glovebox. Papers, lots of them. Pens, probably don't work. Headphones, a DVD. Gum. I took the gum out, it was stale. I unwrapped a few of the pieces and set them on the dashboard.

I lifted the heavy bottle of rum and tilted the plastic rim into my mouth. It burned. The rum burned its way all the way down my throat to my nauseous stomach. I pulled the bottle back.

Oh God, that was terrible. I wanted to gag. I picked up a piece of gum and started chewing it. It didn't really help, well after a few seconds it did. I think it was more my saliva building up.

Again. I took the gum out, swigged, and replaced the gum with another piece. Oh God that shit is awful!

I put the bottle down and picked up the pen and notepad. Where do I start? You can't come up with this stuff on the fly. I don't even know how long it's been since I've written a regular letter. Just write anything, it doesn't matter.

"FUCK IT."

No, you can't start with cuss words. Or maybe you can? Well, I don't want to. I turned to a clean sheet of paper.

"I CANT DO THIS ANYMORE."

That's better. Now, what can't you do?

"I CANT HANDLE THIS LIFE."

What about this life?

"I CANT JUGGLE, I CANT KEEP UP, I'M FAILING, NOT DOING THINGS RIGHT."

You're writing too much. Start over. Another large drink of rum and piece of gum. A new sheet of paper.

"I CANT DO THIS ANYMORE. EVERYTHING IS FALLING APART."

Good. I'm starting to get a little buzzed. Well, that's what happens when you drink on an empty stomach. I laughed. Where was I? Ok, what exactly is 'everything'?

"MY JOB CAREER, MY WIFE, MY FAMILY."

Go ahead. Say it. They're going to find out anyway.

"MY AFFAIR."

Ok, ok. Don't cross it out. Keep going. I took another drink. Should I attack them? Can I cuss out Christina in my suicide note? Try it.

"FUCK YOU CHRISTINA."

Well, what if they find you. No, no, not an option. They won't find

167

me. I'm going far away. I'm leaving. I took all the cash I had out of my wallet. It wasn't much but it would be enough to get a bus ticket or a small meal somewhere. I'm going to have to hitchhike. No one will pick me up. Now that I think about it, I don't want any witnesses anyway. That would ruin everything, if some guy came to the police saying he picked up a hitchhiker near the bridge last night and there was no body in the water.

Back to the letter.

Ok, mentation something about each one.

"MY CAREER IS GOING NOWHERE, I'M GOING BACKWARD, LOSING MY JOB. I HATE IT. I HATE EVERYTHING ABOUT MY CAREER. IT WAS A MISTAKE. ITS TOO LATE FOR ME TO CHANGE."

I started getting angry at myself.

"I HATE IT."

I hit the dashboard with my fist. That felt good. It felt good to get intense right now. That's what I need. I need to lose control. To get in the moment. I hit it again. Harder, you don't have to care about breaking anything.

"I HATE MY FUCKING JOB. MY COWORKERS. MY CUBICLE. ITS MINDLESS. I FEEL POINTLESS. A WASTE OF A LIFE. I WILL NEVER BE HAPPY OR SATISFIED."

Good. Let it out. I took another drink and hit the dash again. It was burning less and the hitting was better than a gum chaser.

"CHRISTINA . FUCK YOU."

It felt so good writing.

"FUCK YOU. FUCK YOU. FUCK YOU. I HATE YOU. FUCK

YOU. YOURE DESTROYING ME. FUCK YOU! FUCK!"

God I hope she reads this.

Drink. Hit. Drink. Hit.

"FUCK YOU CHRISTINA!"

I wrote it real big on a piece of paper. She has to see this.

"YOU'RE A FUCKING IDIOT. A USER. YOU DIDNT HAVE TO DO THIS TO ME. WHY ME? WHY ME? WHAT DID I DO TO YOU? I NEVER HURT YOU? FUCK YOU. I ACTUALLY TREATED YOU NICE. WAS GOOD TO YOU. AND HOW DO YOU REPAY ME.   BY   SETTING   ME   UP.   BLACKMAILING   ME. THREATENING ME. I'M NOT FALLING FOR IT. I WANT EVERYONE TO KNOW. YOU USED ME. I DID NOT WANT THE KID. I TRIED TO GET AN ABORTION."

I don't care if the kid grows up one day and reads this. It needs to know it has a shitty mother.

"FUCK YOU. I NEVER WOULD HAVE FUCKED YOU IF I WASNT DRUNK."

That's a lie. but say it anyway. Lets see her argue with a missing dead man.

Now. Now Melanie.

"MELANIE."

"MELANIE. MELANIE. MELANIE. MELANIE"

What do I say? Mean? Nice? How do I feel?

"MELANIE. I'M SORRY. I'M SORRY SO MANY TIMES. I NEVER THOUGHT THINGS WOULD END UP LIKE THIS. I LOVE YOU. I LOVE YOU SO MUCH. WHAT HAPPENED TO US?"

I started crying. Another drink. I'm buzzed. I might even be drunk? I hit the dash and cried harder.

"FUCK. I LOVED YOU AND EVERYTHING FELL APART. I MISS THE OLD US. I KNOW IT WILL NEVER COME BACK. I MISS THE GOOD TIMES. WE DONT HAVE GOOD TIMES ANYMORE. ALL WE DO IS FIGHT. I'M SORRY. I NEVER MEANT TO HURT YOU. I DIDNT WANT TO CHEAT ON YOU."

It's true.

"I JUST DIDNT KNOW WHAT TO DO. I HAVE LOW-SELFESTEEM. I NEEDED TO FEEL LOVED. I DONT FEEL LIKE YOU LOVE ME ANYMORE. I DONT KNOW WHAT ELSE TO DO. PLEASE FORGIVE ME. I'M SORRY. I'M SORRY."

Now the kids. This is easy. I don't even know them. Don't say that. You care. Of course you care. You're just detached. For the first time, I'm feeling really sorry for them. Don't feel sorry. You're a bad father. You should have never been a father. And now you have a third offspring coming. Oh God. You're so messed up. Look at you. What have you done? What did you do? I drank and hit some more.

"CHILDREN. I'M SORRY."

Don't say anything else. There's nothing you can say. I looked at the bottle of booze. I had drunken a lot. Have cars been driving by this whole time? I laughed while I cried.

"God!" I yelled. It felt intense. I yelled again, "Fuck!"

"Fuck you! Fuck you God!" I yelled at the top of my lungs and punched the car. I pounded my fist on the dash over and over while I yelled.

"Fuck you Christina! I'm so sorry Melanie! I'm sorry! I'm fucking sorry! Kids," tears were pouring out of my face. "I'm sorry kids. I'm no good. I'm not good." Good, what does that even mean?

"Good," I said the word while I sobbed all over the steering wheel and the notepad. "Good. Bad. Good."

Just words. Is there even a difference. Why am I thinking this?

"I'm sorry, I'm sorry," I said the words over and over while I cried all over myself.

What am I supposed to do?

There's no plan. I'm drunk as hell. I'm spilling booze all over myself. I can't think straight. I'm going off on tangents. I'm staring out the window at passing cars. They have their own life. They're going home to happy lives. They have good jobs. I'll never be like them. I'll never have what they have. They don't know me. I don't know myself. I feel like a teenager. I let my head fall against the window.

I banged it. Harder. I banged my head against the window harder. I yelled and banged it hard! Harder! Harder! Louder!

The glass broke. Was I bleeding? No. I don't think so. There was glass on me. I don't care. I grabbed the steering wheel with both hands and started shaking it. Trying to rip it off the dash.

You have ruined everything. Everything you are, you could ever be. I grabbed the rum bottle by the neck and smacked it around the dash. Banging it like a mallet. I took the pens from the glove box and started stabbing the interior. I ripped holes in the seat. The pens bent on the dash. I tried to carve 'sorry' on the dash. I pulled on the seat belt and cried. Oh God I cried so hard. My throat was falling apart from yelling so much. I pulled my hair. I clenched my jaw. My eyes were hurting. I bit the seat belt and yelled. What am I supposed to do?

"What the fuck am I supposed to do?" I yelled out the broken window. I grabbed the blinker knob and broke it off. I banged the rum bottle on the glove box door till it broke. Ripped the papers. Threw them. Fuck.

"What am I supposed to do? What? What? What?" I took my keys out of the ignition and stared at them. I held the jagged edge of one of the keys against my arm. "What?" I dragged it across my forearm. Nothing happened. No mark. What was I expecting.

I drank more rum. I let it spill all over myself.

I tried the keys on my arm again. It burned. I did it again and again. clawing at my tightened forearm with my keys. I started seeing red. Red lines appeared. Blood. It hurt and felt so good. I didn't want to stop. What's wrong with you?

I picked up the notepad and started tearing the pages out. I ripped up all the stuff I had written. Fuck this! You don't belong here. Not anymore.

Get the fuck out of this town. Out now!

I opened the car door. I am drunk. Fast. I need it for support. I'm going to fall over.

I pushed my seat forward. Leave. Take the bike out. Wrestle it out. Spiderwebs. Is it leaving marks? You care. Don't leave tracks. Muddy?

I can't walk. I can barely see straight. I'm half using the bike for support. Ok, this might not work out right. Flat tires.

I started walking to the bridge with the bike. Ok. Ok. focus.

How does this work? I slid down a hill or something. It's dark.

It's easier to crawl. I'm not blacking out. I'm trying not to. Everything is passing strange. Time. I have to piss.

Ok, focus. Don't fuck this up.

What's the point. I let myself piss my pants.

I need to drop articles. Clothing. I shouldn't have gotten drunk. Mistake.

I'm going. I'm making it. There's more bushes than I thought. I'm probably getting torn up. Do I care?

I don't remember. I was throwing up. Melanie. I'm sorry.

I don't have the bike anymore. Shit. It's ok, get it afterward.

It's easier to walk on the bridge. I hope a car doesn't come by.

Spit. Stand. Don't stand. I'm so sorry. Breath. You can't.

Drop things. Drop and leave. Shoes are good. Shirt?

I'm not laughing anymore. Was I ever?

After. I drop things. I need to hide. A few hours. I have to hide the bike.

I shouldn't have gotten drunk. Who cares.

That's blood. What have I done to myself, my life.

I don't care if this doesn't make sense. Not a good plan. They'll never find me.

It's getting harder to think. I think I am blacking out? I have puke all over my shirt.

Focus. Focus. I tried to stand up straight. I have to hold the rail.

Fresh air. No good. Good.

Why am I doing this? Is this real? Really happening?

Walk. Walk. Closer. How far? The middle. Why?

Lean. Ok. Look. It's dark. There's water down there.

Take off your shoe. Shoes. Ok, look. Down there.

Drop one. Two.

173

Shirt? Who cares? Why not?

Drop it. It's cold.

Want over now.

Puke.

Can't yell. Weak.

Railing, lean. Air. Wind.

Cold? Wind.

Dark. Water.

Sorry. I'm sorry.

Crying.

Sorry.

Fuck career.

Fuck Christina.

Fuck Melanie.

Fuck me.

Fuck people.

Sorry kids.

Kids matter. Nothing else.

Sorry. Wind. Water.

Stare. Time.

Now hide. Hide.

Crawl back. Focus. Find bike. Blood.

Stare. Time.

Time.

-SEVEN-

Sleep deprived. Malnourished. Emotionless. Indifferent. Calm. Drugged. I feel drugged still. My body still moving against my will. It's that old saying "It's got a mind of it's own". Thanks. I'm conscious, I'm thinking. I'm self aware. I think therefore I am. I fucking exist, but my body, it's got an existence of it's own.

I'm in front of the lobby elevators now. First in line. I didn't, my body didn't, push any buttons but I can see the elevator lights counting towards zero, -21, -20, -19. Are those negative numbers?

The lights got closer to zero, then the doors opened. Me and a handful of others marched in silently. Our heels clicking on the hard floor the only sound. The ceiling inside the elevator is high, higher than any I've ever been in before. I could see the buttons on the walls light up. Square buttons, each with a negative number, covered every surface of the elevator. Thousands of them. A handful of buttons lit up on their own.

One for each of us I'm assuming.

Then it drops. The thing sinks quick and I can feel my body lighten and want to lift off the floor. Each stop is hard, but my body stays ridged.

Every time the elevator slows, and the doors open, we're faced with a glossy white wall and a white noise. Like the sound of an air conditioner or the inside of an airplane. One of us steps out and then the door shuts, leaving the rest of us in the tall narrow elevator with the dim button lights to feel weightless again.

About half of us are gone when I feel my body tighten up. Next stop is mine. I just know somehow. The lift stops on the negative 112th floor. The doors open, bright wall, same white noise.

It was here that I left my body. Or didn't really leave it, but got that strange sensation when you feel like you're watching yourself in a movie. I watched myself, my body, walk out the elevator and step out toward the white wall. My body turned and faced the unimaginable. The elevator closed behind me and left me facing a personal horror. A sight similar to one I have had to witness day after day after day, for years. But this was unreal. This was on another scale. Unbelievable. A vision of terror I never would have expected. A massive open room with no end in sight, filled with cells. An open area bigger than any stadium dome, hanger or warehouse. Small rectangular cells form a grid along the vast floor.

I knew what those cells with short walls were. I knew what was in each cell without even looking. I am staring at a space big enough to fit an entire downtown city, instead of buildings and streets, it's filled with office cubicles. Hundreds, thousands, tens of thousands? The sound, oh dear God I know what that sound is.

They were personal cubicles and each cube contained an individual working. Working feverishly away at some unseen project. Typing, almost madly at keyboards. Filling the large space with thousands upon thousands of quick little keyboard clicks creating the steady cloud of noise overhead. I just watched myself put one foot in front of the other and start walking into the city of cubicles in a very calm, and I'm sure waxed faced, manner.

If I had it my way, I would have spun around and pounded the elevator buttons to return up. Or would I? Where would I go? But my body had it's own agenda. Instead my body moved itself forward, down one of the corridors and past a row of cubicles. I've spent the better part of two decades in one of these things. I can sense them without looking. I don't need to see it. I can feel it. It's in my senses, not by blood, but years of forced exposure. Trips to the kitchen for coffee refills, unneeded bathroom breaks, step outside cell phone calls.

All occupied by some bleach white collared worker, typing away. Men and women sitting in ergonomic chairs with L shaped desks, in cubicles barely big enough to stretch your arms. Pens, pencils, staplers, keyboards, monitors, phones, tangled wires, pads of paper, paper clips, waste baskets, coffee mugs, stiff carpet, plastic desktop liners, overhead cabinets, fluorescent lighting, pin boards, fake plants, family photos, manilla folders, calendars, benefit packages, open enrollment and holiday dates circled, contact lists, antiglare screens, single celled comics, employee handouts, flowcharts, org charts, Gantt charts, white out, breath mints, tupperware lunches.

I know the exact contents down to the soft padded pin cushion lining on the wall, like a corporate padded cell. It's unsettling. A haven and at the same time a dreaded, despised micro-environment. Like a cage. It become yours. A place to think. Your sanctuary. You look forward to it when you are away and trapped at home with a nonsexual, cold frigid wife and disrespectful immature needy kids. And hate, loath the place when you're stuck in it at work for the next eight hours. Of course since you pretty much live in the thing, you do everything in there. Eat, groom, pick your nose, fart, scribble notes and goals for a better life, contemplate if you can get yourself off without getting caught.

I'd go into mine nearly every morning with coffee tasting like Band-aids and just space out. It was like stepping into a physical representation of my mind. A thought chamber. My own think tank flooded in fluorescent lights. I can relax, stare blankly at the monitor. I can get tense and take my anger out by stapling repeatedly, breaking writing instruments. Fantasize about fucking the secretary, or any of the woman in the office. All of them. Especially the ones in stockings. I can engage in little masochistic acs to make the day go faster. Nothing bad could happen to me in there. Work, work I can handle. But I could never get diagnosed with cancer, get in a car accident, lose my home, get into a fight with my wife. I was protected from the outside world in my cube and at the same time it wasted my life and destroyed me.

This was familiar territory, and my expected destiny.

I've made too many turns in this maze of cubes to get my bearings straight from the elevator. I'm totally disoriented. I tried to calculate how many are down here it in my head and couldn't. Too hard to guess how many cubicles are down each corridor when you can't see the end of the row. The sounds, the noise. It's overwhelming. Like being in a massive insect hive of human workers. Instead of millions of insect mouths and parts consuming microscopic particles, it's human digits extending and contracting, clicking away at plastic keys with letters and numbers. I wanted to cover my ears, but of course I can't move a muscle willingly. I'm a slave to this body. It's not my own anymore. A stranger trapped in familiar flesh. Everything it does, it does on it's own. It's own intentions. It's own agenda, it's own will. My thoughts are simply along for the ride it seems.

I feel like I've had dose after dose of antidepressants. My body is calm, but my mind is active. Nervously curious and accepting of anything that might be around the next hallway. Put the human mind through enough shit and it adapts. Adapts to take any form of shit. Destroy his job. Take away any chance at intelligent offspring. Even fail the man at marriage, mating, fucking the mistress. And you've broken him. I've been through enough.

And I walked past these cubicles, hundreds of them. A maze, a massive cubicle city within a city. I imagined myself a microscopic bacteria in a petri dish, obstacles everywhere. My legs just kept walking on their own, I just kept watching, unable to react.

What are they working on, typing? I'm straining the muscles around my eyes, trying to see inside the mini offices as I walk past. I'm tensing up. It's too difficult. But I keep trying with each passing cube. My eyes are burning in their sockets, my ears ringing, eye muscles strained.

If I can't see inside the cubicles perfectly, I'll focus on the near deafening sound. I tune into the white noise and let it become clearer. My ear drum, hammer, anvil. Cilia capturing the vibrations, transferring to an auditory nerve and delivering it to my mind. My mind automatically does all the work. Millions of years of evolution to design the perfect organic microphone. I walk further down the hall and all the sounds I'm realizing are human. Incoherent, but human. It's not a language, no. I'm not picking up any words. But definitely human. Not plastic keyboard clicks like I thought. It's sounding more like screams. Yes, yells. Cries. These are painful screams I'm hearing. There are so many happening constantly it's hard to pick up. But some are getting clearer as I go deeper down the corridors.

I'm able to peak around the cubicle walls slightly. I can hear the sounds directly. Isolated gasps and yells coming from each cube as I pass it. I can sometimes see a shadow in the cubicle. A human figure. One sitting. The next one standing.

Each passing cube give me a little more detail, a better perspective. The figures inside appear they way I expected. Mostly men, all dressed in business attire. Mostly sitting, haunched over a desk, they seem to be working. But closer inspection they are in torturous positions. Terrifying poses. Strapped to their modern looking office chairs. Engaged not only in tedious pencil pushing work, but devastating actions. Sick twisted, you might say disgusting actions. I can't be sure, but I want to say some of the people are bleeding. I'm noticing most had large splotches of blood on their clothes. Some were bleeding profusely from various wounds. Every single cubicle occupied with a tortured body.

What the fuck is going on here? I'm panicking. I'm feeling that numbness wear off. The drugged feeling, it's slipping. Whatever it is is wearing off. That comforting accepting drugged drunk feeling is slipping. The poison is leaving my veins and being replaced with adrenaline and fear. A control panel of dials in my mind are moving. Needles are twitching from curious to anxious, from calm to terror. My body is still moving on it's own. Answering to another nervous system. I don't have control of myself, or my destiny. It's all predetermined. Every step, every breath. Probably even these thoughts. They aren't my own. All the human thoughts that have occurred and will ever pass through human minds is already determined. By what? A God? Gods? Nature? It's all set somewhere. Even the fragments of my mind and body I think I have control of I probably don't.

My body stopped walking. My mind kept racing.

The slim entrance of a cubicle, just big enough to push a file cabinet through. Plain, white, generic. Just like all the others in the subterranean tortured city around me.

I went inside. The walls and desk were clean, white, sterile. There was a small steel chair, looked like it was welded out of scrap metal. A computer, black. Telephone, black. Clock, all black no numbers, hands pointed to where 1:06 should be. Small white bottles, ink? Pens lined up perfectly along the desk, I'm assuming all black. Stacks of white papers. A calendar with the sixth of January circled. No year listed. The perfect black and white Howard Hughes desk, minus the tetanus infested looking chair. My body took a seat, and my mind slipped right back into where it belonged. Home.

I looked at the monitor in front of me. I tried to move my head to the left, wouldn't budge. Still no control. I could feel the metal under my body. Hard, cold steel. A complete ergonomic disaster.

I sat there motionless. Still with my thoughts. The clock is moving too fast for a normal clock. I can hear the people in the offices next to me. Something that sounds a lot like slapping, and a popping sound.

Just watching everything unfold. Like some kind of story. A personal story, written just for me and I'm the main character. There's a plot, I'm sure. But it's not exactly clear. So I just watch, and accept everything that was happening.

And it continued this way. Unwillingly confined to my chair. What's controlling my arms and hands? My sub-conscious? An evil spirit? Was I possessed? After everything I had been through I didn't doubt it. I would still say I was dreaming, but even if I was, it didn't matter.

I felt my neck muscles tighten, and slowly start turning my head to the side. When it stopped I could see my reflection through a mirror on the wall. From the neck up I was an expressionless face. My eyes calm and trance-like. Below the neck, I was half undressed. The desk lamp had somehow turned and was stretched out over my torso. My layers of shirts and clothing unbuttoned and spread apart. My chest was so pale it almost glowed under the light.

I accept the fact that my right hand decide to move. To reach out and grab one of the many bottles from the desk, the other hand instinctively opened the cap. My arms moved mechanically, my hands like claws. The bottle tilted down toward me and I watched the clear contents spill out onto my chest. Felt the cool sensation of liquid, then smelled the strongest odor of isopropanol. It grew more intense and made me dizzy, but I kept breathing deep and calm. I could feel my throat begin to burn. The hands stopped pouring and set the bottle down. The dizziness lingered but began to fade.

I'm just the character in a story.

Still observing through the mirror, I could see one hand reach for an object on the desk and hand it to my other hand. The way a nurse would hand a surgeon astringent. I hold the object up in front of my eyes. It's a pen. My left hand raised and pinched the cap to take it off. I'm staring at the brass tip of the pen. I can see the ink forming a small bead on the tip. My arm moves the pen closer to my eye. I can see the imperfections in the brass tip, minuscule scratches left over from the machine that shaped it on the factory line no doubt. The pen moves closer, it's out of focus now. Just a blurry object in front of the intense white light glowing down from above.

The pen touched my eye. I know this, because I can feel it. Its awkward and uncomfortable. It's irritating the surface, but not hurting, yet. I want to say my heart is pounding harder and I'm getting sweaty and shaking. The dials in my mind are getting faster readings. The needles flickering towards the red 'danger' numbers.

I suspected my hand's intention with the pen. Not enough control, or even the reflexes, to wince or recoil. But I knew what was next. The hand raised the pen away from my eye and moved towards my chest.

I wanted to squirm.

I wanted to yell.

The hand lowered.

I wanted to shut my eyes.

The pen hovering above my chest. Teasing.

Scream! Yell! Kick!

The pen lowered slowly. I stared unblinking in the mirror. Eyes still wide and calm. Stop. Stop yourself! The dizziness completely gone and replaced with anticipation and horror. Adrenaline raced through every vein and neuron in my flesh. My brain was drowning in it. The control panel in my mind, out of control. Dials spun wildly, meters flicked back and forth. Red lights flashing.

Stop myself!

The tip of the pen touched. I felt the hard tip press down on my sternum. Stop! Blink! Close! I tried sending verbal commands. The pen kept pressing downwards. I felt the tiny spot of pressure grow. Don't, don't do it. The spot began to ache, and just like that, quickly the surgeon hand jerked the pen downward, pressing the pen deep into my skin. A slice that extended from my chest to my stomach.

I recoiled in my mind. I watched and expected blood to come up, but only the sensation of a burning line of pain. I wanted to scream. I tried. But my mouth continued to breath calmly. The yells were trapped in my head. The surgeon hand rose and moved back to my sternum slowly. Then again it lowered and dragged the pen hard and deep into my torso.

Yell! Stop! Yell!

No control. I hyperventilated in my mind. Imagining myself breathing in and out quickly. Imagining my body shutting down and preparing itself to slip unconscious. Only it didn't. It wouldn't. I stayed conscious and continued to stare uncontrollably. My cubicle converted into a small operating room and me the patient, the nurse and the surgeon.

The line burned from below my neck to my stomach. The surgeon hand moved faster and pressed harder while I stared. Yells flooded my head and the pain kept growing. I knew it was coming but it still brought me to complete shock when it happened. The red line in my body grew deeper and darker. I could feel it tearing. Not only feel it tearing but watch it. Little by little the skin on my chest began to separate. Dark red blood began to seeping out of the line. I yelled, I screamed. The surgeon hand kept digging into me. The nurse hand grabbed for papers on the desk and began blotting at the gashing wound. Soaking up blood and dropping the papers to the floor. The surgeon hand continued to cut till nothing was left to hold my skin together.

With an expression calm as a t.v. hypnotized four year old, I watched my torso split open. The screams in my head intense. The wound spread apart. Vision. Sight, coming and going. My mind wanted to faint but wouldn't. It lingered on the edge of consciousness. Absorbing the sensations of pain I have never felt before.

Oh God. Oh God. I'm begging. Oh God. Not even for anything. Just begging. Oh God.

The surgeon dropped the pen, the nurse dropped the blood soaked papers. Each hand grabbed at a side of the wound and pulled. The tearing sensation. The feeling of my own hands reaching into my body and pulling my organs to the sides. I wasn't even begging anymore. Borderline shock.

Neck tightening again. My head turned, twisting away from the mirror. It pointed upward toward the impossibly high ceiling of fluorescent light. My neck muscles kept contracting, stretching out and downward. Positioning my head so I could view right down into my open body cavity. I was looking straight into the wound. Inches away from the bloody horror.

The hands still pulling unrecognizable organs and tissue apart. Nothing looked familiar, like the stuff you see in anatomy books or doctor's office posters. But then. Then. Now. Now I. I don't know what to think. I am flooded with pain. Watching my hands slowly pull more. And more organs aside. Aside to reveal. A face. Not just any face. I am mad. Mad with pain and confusion.

The greatest and most bizarre nightmare I could never had imagined. I am staring right at Melanie. My son and daughter. Christina's face is there too, covered in thick dark red. The faces. Raw and sickly. But it's them. Eye's closed. Their heads in my torso framed by intestines, ribs and lungs. Just like another one of the organs. I didn't know how to react. What to think. Pain must still be there but overshadowed by shock. I stared directly at their asleep looking faces mixed in with my guts. Then they woke up.

First Melanie. Then the boy. The girl. Finally Christina. One by one their eyelids split open slowly. Eyelashes like sickly venus flytraps. Bright white eyes, dark pupils in a pool of red. Even stranger, their mouths opened. Yawn like. Eyebrows slowly flexing. Jaws stretching. Eyes blinking. They all looked directly at me.

My daughter started weeping. Her eyes glazed over and tears ran out. Her mouth made a whimpering sound. Melanie's face, her eyes concerned looked over at our daughter. The boy began to cry. Melanie slowly shifted her eyes to him, then to me.

I could see my family staring at me, eyes full of pain. Even Melanie began tearing up. Her eyes so sad, almost begging. No more sensation of pain. I was now in a trance staring directly at my family.

Stop. Stop. I said it softly in my head. I wanted to use my hands to hold my son and daughter's head. To stroke their hair and calm them. The kids sobbing hard now. Even Melanie begging to cry. She began biting her lip. Something I haven't seen her do in ages. Only when she is in severe emotional pain.

Please. Their eyes were begging. I'm sorry. I know I've hurt you. Their eyes said it all. Abandoned. I know I've left you, I'm sorry. I didn't know what else to do. I lost control of everything. I didn't know how to solve it. My problems. Melanie was pouring tears.

I wasn't begging for God anymore, but for their forgiveness. I can do better, I know I can. It's in me. I don't want to abandon you. I want to fix things. I can make it better. You are my family. My flesh and blood. I can fix this.

I was looking deep into the souls of their eyes. Of the faces that affected me and I impacted the most. This was the life I had chosen. The offspring I willingly had and even more important than marriage, obligated, committed myself to caring and protecting. My son, my oldest own flesh and blood. It was my job to raise him with values I have learned myself. I needed to be selfless. Committed. Strong for them. They come first. Until I can't do it any longer. But will not quit by choice.

Their eyes begged me to come back. Melanie's eyes sadder than I have ever seen. She begged me to come home. Honest apologetic eyes. Sad and helpless. I can make it better Melanie. We are a team. We promised to be there for each other. I've had the lowest point of my life but you didn't leave me. Her eyes looked at the cold Christina face close to her, then back at me. She told me through her eyes, she understood. She knew about Christina. She knew the whole time, but didn't know how to handle it.

She was upset with herself for not being, what she thought was a good wife. Not being there physically and emotionally for me. She apologized over and over. Said her self-esteem crumbled after the boy.

She felt it was all her fault. We consoled each other and promised we could recover. We could do it, heal. We could repair everything.

It was a breakthrough like we never had before. I felt connected to her again. A family. One. But how Melanie? I don't understand where I am or how I leave? How did I get here? What is all this? I don't care what this place even is, I just want to be home. Back with you and the kids. Repairing, starting over. The things I've seen.

Leave, she begged.

How? I begged.

You are asleep. Past out drunk a mile from the bridge. You are ok. Her eyes were deep and genuine. You need to wake up and come home. Wake up and come back to us.

I stared at her confused.

We are waiting with the police. You didn't do anything wrong. We just want you home safe with us.

What about Christina?

Christina isn't pregnant with your child. She just thinks it's yours. But it's not.

I will! I will wake up. I will come home! Wake up! Wake up I yelled at myself. I visualized my body unconscious in the grass. Vomit all around. Get up! Awaken! I imagined shaking my shoulders.

Christina's eyes opened. My thoughts went quiet. There was a second of silent staring.

She doesn't matter. Wake up! Wake up!

"I am awake," Christina said.

Her voice caught me off guard. I stopped yelling in my head and stared at her. She looked back at me silently. Melanie's eyes continued to cry and long for me. Ignore Christina.

Wake up!

"I told you," Christina looked straight at me.

Not you, me!

"You are too," she said. I watched her lips move.

No I'm not. Melanie help me get up!

Melanie's face just cried and begged.

Christina's eyes looked at Melanie.

Melanie tried to kiss me.

Melanie! Help!

Melanie looked. I looked.

Help me wake up! Melanie just sobbed harder. The kids cried harder. I could hear their cries. Christina stared straight at me. Her face cold. She moved her lips slow. The words hard and her voice serious.

"You. Are. Awake."

No! No! I'm not. Tell her Melanie! Melanie tried to kiss me again. She mouthed 'I love you'. No!

Christina just watched. Why can't I wake up!

Christina's eye's got dark. Very dark.

Oh no. Oh no. She didn't have to say anything. I know. I know without her saying a word. Oh no. No.

No!

No!

God.

God!

God?

What is this! What are you! What am I?

I'm not waking up, I am awake.

This is awake for me now. This is it.

My Epiphany
epiph· a· ny \i-ˈpi-fə-nē\
to manifest, to show
noun

1. The divine being: I stared deep inside myself. There was no divine being in the heavens above or hell below. It was inside me. I am my God. Nature put my flesh and bone together. Meiosis. And kept it together. Mitosis. But it was I who developed my mind into the self-aware existence with a personality that lays here now. I gave myself the ability to make choices and decisions for my body. I created who I was. I created my purpose. My reason for existence.

2. The realization: I stared deep inside myself. A mind with the ability to make choices for the body. I saw the life, the actions I had chosen. I chose to marry Melanie. To have two children. To sleep with Christina. I chose to fall out of the sky. I decided to walk down the street with the others. I chose my career. I found my way to my cubicle. All on my own. There were no drugs. No invisible force controlling me. I brought myself here. I did this to myself. There is no one, nothing else to blame.

My Epiphany.

The eyes were black and empty. Endless. The creator, the decision maker and now the punisher. Face to face with my own problems. My internal problems fully exposed. My demons. Sometimes a job can destroy a man. Sometimes it's a woman. Sometime's it's financial responsibilities or a child. For me, all of those things destroyed me.

I would not let myself go. I would not let myself have another chance. I had my chance. All the opportunities I gave myself and destroyed. My inner turmoil, debates, confusion.

I was in control and always had been.

My nausea intensified. I dry heaved and felt my gut suck in.

Even if I could wake up, I would never let myself.

I was in control and always had been. I've chosen to destroy myself and all my opportunities.

Why. Why would a human do this to himself? Guilt? How far back does this go? Have I sabotaged myself from the start? From childhood? It's been one setup for failure after another. I've let myself go on too long and now I was ending it.

The black eyes were fixed on mine.

I wasn't unconscious in a bush. I knew what happened. I knew the choice I made. I chose to take my shoes off on that bridge. Chose to throw them over the edge. I wanted to turn and walk away toward freedom. But even more, I wanted to stand barefoot up on that ledge and look down. I watched my shoes in the water down below. They floated so slow and peaceful. I watched them sink and disappear into the dark water. I chose to follow them at the last minute. It was so easy standing there. So effortless. I only had to step forward once and let myself fall. Disappear. Nothing was fake about it. .

I felt my arm again. Felt all my limbs.

I willfully turned my head toward the desk. My desk.

I looked at my pens, papers, instruments.

I picked up one of my pens. I used my arm, I had control. I sat up in my chair. Laid my left arm down on my desk in front of me. I stabbed my arm with my pen. A popping sound. I did it again. I could scream if I wanted. Could yell and not just in my head. I stabbed. A trail of dark dots appeared.

Tears started coming out.

This was my choice. My will. It always was.

I sat in my cubicle, and let myself destroy myself.

-END IT-

-BODY COMPANY-

The afterlife. It's not what I was told. There's no spiritual world the parapsychologist spoke of. No heaven men in robes spoke of. No long twisting line with a sign reading: Reincarnation. Not even a ghostly soul to stare through.

So. I'm alone.

Not like the loneliness of being in a room by yourself. Or home on a Friday night. Not like the loneliness of being quiet in a corner at a crowded party. Or being single for decades. Not like an only child. Not the same loneliness of being stranded or detached from society in cabin. Not even like solitary confinement in a prison cell or mental hospital. Not like the loneliness of being a brain, a mind with your own cranium home, that no one can ever enter and invade your own private thoughts.

It's a different kind of alone. Something I've never felt before. I don't even have a body to share my commands with. No fingers or hands I can make twitch or flex upon thought. No eyes to look out of, to intercept spectrums of light. No flesh to house nerve endings to pick up sensations. No ears to trap waves of sound, vibrating molecules and canals to channels the sound down dark twisted paths to miniature bones connected to nerves. No tongue with a bed of tastebuds to push flavors and matter down an esophagus. A fleshy hose for ingesting matter filled with nutrients. No nostrils, tubes, caves for inhaling scents. Smoky warnings or sweet pleasures. No genitals or gonads to keep my genes in the overcrowded pool.

No senses to interpret an environment around me. To survive and reproduce. On earth all my senses were used for navigating my environment. Protecting me from danger. Predators. Finding food. Survival. Locating a mate. Reproduction. There is no need for that now.

I'm alone. Without the company of my body.

All I have is my memory. A memory filled with childhood visions. A house, a room I grew up in. Names and faces of family and friends, humans that have gone their own way. I don't know if they are alive or dead. Happy or sad. The English language.

And now that's leaving me. I'm forgetting the faces and names. It's getting harder to remember. Even words I used to use everyday to talk to people. To think my way through problems and tasks with an inner monologue. To write these words. To be a thinking, self-aware, conscious being.

It's all slipping. Fading.

I'm dead.

I have left my physical body.

This is the loneliness of a nonexistence. It doesn't matter whether its before or after my birth. It's all the same. A nonexistence.

Forever.

I am alone now.

Eternity.

www.ingramcontent.com/pod-product-compliance
Lightning Source LLC
Chambersburg PA
CBHW020435180626
46812CB00003B/1249